PINKY SWEAR

PINKY SWEAR

KARA STEVENS

For Judy

PROLOGUE

FRIDAY AFTERNOON, JUNE 10TH, LAST
DAY OF SCHOOL, CLIFFS VIEW HIGH
SCHOOL, FINAL SENIOR CLASS PEP
RALLY

I've been waiting a long time to reveal the truth. Now, they sit in the stands right in front of me, still unaware of who they're looking for. Their feet tap the wooden planks beneath and wide eyes dart from side to side as if trying to avoid a predator's attack. But there is no way out. I've got them. The once familiar gray walls of the gymnasium are now covered with banners that bleed crimson and blue. Every inch of this campus is saturated in those school colors. Tacky decorations, like confetti and crate paper, scatter across the floor and a balloon arch is loosely built over the stage. Every few seconds a balloon escapes and floats up to the rafters then "pops," causing everyone to flinch. The band blasts the senior song and the students sing along loudly and out of tune. My ears are ringing. I wish I could turn down the volume or put the celebration on mute. I take a deep breath. It's almost over. In just a few minutes the party will end...and this time there are consequences.

CHAPTER 1

LAST DAY OF SCHOOL, FIRST PERIOD

The Santa Ana winds are unpredictable. Sometimes they arrive out of nowhere, and pierce the skin like a superficial nick from a razor. The winds can whip up a mess and cause a media frenzy of wildfire warnings. For that reason, people often refer to them as the "devil winds" here in Southern California. However, the winds can be gentle with a subtle warmth that wraps around your body as if it's hugging you, like today.

There are moments of stillness throughout Cliffs View High School as Bryn Matthews walks down the long outdoor corridor. She glides her hand across the lockers; the clicking of the metal padlocks chime one after the other, *click clack click clack,* in perfect unison with her footsteps. When she walks the campus with her girlfriends, combined with their persistent giggling, there's no way to ignore the trio as they make their way through the halls. Walking with purpose, they call it, a "here we come, get out of the way" sort of strut. Another abrupt breeze causes one of the straps of Bryn's yellow sundress to fall slightly off her slim shoulder, leaving a trail of goose bumps in its wake. She walks past the rows of identical classrooms and looks at the students who start to trickle inside, catching a glimpse of her own somber reflection in the window. It's the last morning of high school, and it feels bittersweet to Bryn. Bryn is early to class. She always is. Two people are in the room, Mr. Turner, and Mr. Huxley, or "Luke;" he's the teaching assistant and likes the students to call him by his first name. Bryn still feels strange calling him that. Mr. Turner is minutes away from retirement, close to seventy years old, and looks tired all the time. His eyes are frozen in a permanent squint right on the verge of shutting.

Mr. Turner sits in a creaky chair at his desk in the back of the room, blocked off from the rest of the class. Piles of books and messy folders stack up around his desk, forming a barricade that he hides behind. Most of the day it's like he's not there at all. Then he rustles a bit, pops his head up and his bushy gray eyebrows peek out above the clutter. Sprouting throughout those massive brows are spiky sharp hairs that angle in all different directions. When he yawns, it looks as if one is going to pop off and shoot across the room like an arrow.

Bryn sits in her seat, waves to Mr. Turner, and watches Luke move his bike to the side of the room. Luke bikes to work every day. Then he either runs on the track or swims laps in the pool. Luke likes to talk about how he is training for a triathlon. Cliffs View High is the perfect place for him; the school values athletics and has put a lot of money into the facilities on campus. After he secures his bike, Luke grabs a basket and walks toward Bryn.

"You know the rules—drop your cell phone."

Bryn smiles and hands over the device. The school's policy: no cell phones in class. Luke takes the basket, hangs it by the door, and scans the room, looking at all the empty seats. "What do you think, is it just going to be you and me today, Miss Matthews? Jessa and Aly did throw quite a fit this week when they heard the news."

Jessa Price and Aly Lockwood are Bryn's best friends. Bryn looks out the window and bites her lower lip. "They'll be here."

Luke walks closer to Bryn, grabs a chair, then flips it around and sits facing her. He crosses his arms around the back of the chair and rests his chin between his palms. "You don't sound convinced."

Bryn fidgets a bit. The truth is that she's not 100 percent sure they'll show up. Typically, the last Friday of school is "Senior Ditch Day." The seniors take a day off from school and throw a party. Last week, the school announced new guidelines for class attendance and a big punishment if anyone was caught at a party: NO GRADUATING. Because of the increase in underage drinking, drunk driving accidents, and public drunkenness, this is the year the school administrators decided to stop looking the other way when it came to the tradition of Senior Ditch Day.

But how did they get the students to come to school at all? That was easy; the only other thing everyones been talking about these last couple of weeks, besides Ditch Day, is the new "Cliffs View Video Yearbook." The film club received a large donation to create a new digital yearbook. The audiovisual room is decked out with all the latest top-of-the-line editing software, resembling the "behind the scenes" area of a film set. The video yearbook is like their own reality show shot on campus. So, the principal decided not to release the yearbook until everyone attended the last day of school and the final farewell pep rally. To add a little less dread to the day, she announced that in each period they would run a portion or "episode" of the video in class. Basically, anyone who wants their copy must attend all their classes, and the final pep rally, and sign out at the end of the day. Now, of course, there are some students who don't care about seeing themselves and all their friends in the Virtual Yearbook. But most of the students are curious and want to get a preview of their fifteen minutes of fame.

"Well, hopefully you'll make it through today unscathed," Luke says. He points toward the window. "There they are."

Bryn ignores his sarcasm. "Told you they'd be here," she says.

At the front of a cluster of students dragging

themselves into the classroom, mumbling about "how messed up this is," are Jessa and Aly. They're dressed for a dramatic entrance. Bryn didn't expect anything less. When the announcement was first made, Jessa took a stand to organize a type of coup, saying, "They can't do this to our party. It has to be illegal to make us come to school on the last day! I'll talk to my father!" Jessa's dad is a top defense attorney—scratch that, *the* top defense attorney in town. She likes to play that card as much as possible.

Luke mumbles to himself, *"you got to be kidding me"* when he sees their outfits. Jessa and Aly are dressed head to toe in all black. They wear wide-brimmed hats, with mesh veils covering their faces, the kind you see a widow wearing at a funeral. They walk into the classroom with their heads down, bowing over a box of Kleenex, dramatically wiping fake tears.

"Obviously we are in mourning," Jessa says. She lifts her veil. "They killed our party."

"Murderers!" Aly says. Her accusation is taking it a little too far. The other students clap and high-five Jessa and Aly while complimenting them on their creative protest.

Jessa stops in front of Bryn. "Don't worry, we brought you a matching hat too." Jessa reaches in her bag and pulls out a black hat for Bryn. She places it on top of Bryn's head, smoothing her thick curls underneath. Bryn's hair is the color of warm honey and tumbles down to the middle of her back. "Perfect!" Jessa says. Aly looks over and smiles at Bryn, giving her a nod of approval, then turns her wide eyes to Luke standing by the TV.

"Alright, *Lukey*, we're here," Aly says. She likes to flirt and use pet names for the T.A.s—especially, in her words, "the hot ones." "Let's get this show on the road!"

"Right on it, Miss Lockwood."

Aly rolls her eyes. "Whatever, hurry up please."

Mr. Turner shuffles in his chair. It's like sometimes you really do forget he's there until you hear that obnoxious throat-clearing thing he does. He manages to get a few words out before coughing. "Go ahead and start the damn thing!"

Bryn turns to Jessa and adjusts her hat. "How long are we going to wear these? It's really itchy," she says.

Jessa shrugs. "I think we made our point." She throws her hat in the air. "Woo hoo! I'm practicing for tomorrow."

Aly sits in the row next to Bryn and Jessa. She follows Jessa's lead and tosses her hat graduation style. Bryn doesn't like to draw too much attention to herself, so she just puts the hat under her chair.

Everyone is anxious to see the footage, but clearly not as excited as Jessa and Aly. Her friends wiggle in their chairs and maneuver themselves into the best position to view the screen. Jessa looks over at Bryn. "Here we go!" She claps and smiles as if the camera is still rolling. Bryn is ready to be free from cameras for a while. She looks over at Luke. He is fumbling with the remote and finally hits play.

The music starts, and student pictures flash onscreen. It's like the intro to a TV show, starring the senior class. Practically everyone cheers as Brad Beckett's picture pops up with a voice-over of his speech before the homecoming football game. Cliffs View lost that game 42 to 6, it was humiliating. The opening clips are creative, with great transitions, from the marching band playing their award-winning songs to water polo and chess matches.

Giggles erupt when video of the powderpuff football game comes up. The senior class girls played the junior class in a game of flag football. It's a tradition, and it's always a disaster. The camera zooms in on a pile of girls tumbling over each other, trying to locate the football. The real funny part is that most of the players touched up their makeup during halftime, without even knowing that is where the name "powderpuff" came from. In the 1950s the players were being ironic, making a joke by staying on the field and powdering their noses; at Cliffs View it is pure vanity. The football fiasco scene ends, but just as the music starts to fade there is a quick disturbance onscreen. The video freezes on a picture of a girl standing on a cliff; the ocean is behind her. The girl looks like a younger Jessa, but the photo is gritty and old, peppered with black-and-white spots.

Bryn turns toward Jessa to ask if it's her but is caught off guard by how Jessa is staring at the screen. It looks like she's in a trance, hypnotized by the strange picture. Jessa grips the desk. Her newly manicured nails dig into the wood, making that horrible sound that causes your whole body to shiver. But Jessa doesn't even seem to notice she is doing it. Then, under her breath, she speaks so quietly Bryn can hardly hear her, *"This must be a joke, how could someone... Who has that picture?"*

Bryn can't make out the rest of what Jessa says. Her words drift off just as the picture disappears from the screen. Bryn can tell she's rattled by it. Jessa's perfect skin has never looked so pale.

Static pops on the screen along with a loud buzzing, as if a swarm of bees are trapped inside. Luke turns down the volume, but heckling from the class takes over and creates even more of a disturbance.

"Hey Luke, that was only a few minutes," Brad says. "It's bad enough we have to be here today, man."

Luke stands in front of the TV, shaking his head. "Sorry, guys, technical difficulties—just give me a second to get it going again." He flicks the lights back on.

The commotion doesn't faze Mr. Turner, who has been asleep since the video began. Each time he snores, the tall stack of paper on his desk shifts with the flow of his heavy breath, causing it to teeter back and forth. His next exhale may just push it over the edge.

Jessa is still staring at the television, which is now black. She stops scratching the desk and starts gnawing at her fingernails. Bryn sees how nervous she is. Jessa usually always keeps it together; she is the epitome of composure. Every detail, from what she wears to school to her makeup and accessories, is flawless. It may sound crazy, but Bryn has never seen her wear the same outfit twice this entire school year. Her home is perfect too. It is exactly where you picture someone like Jessa Price lives. Cliffs View is an affluent area, but most of the homes are older, built in the 1960s, with that rustic beach charm. They may have some exterior "facelifts" or additional square footage but still represent a classic mid-century integrity. Jessa's house has a Hollywood feel to it: brand new, big, and very expensive. Tall palm trees hover over the entrance, and pink tea roses guide you up the pathway to the patio deck. The front double doors look like they belong in an art gallery. They are covered with hundreds of mosaic glass pieces in sky blue, green, and fiery orange that link together, forming an intricate design of a sunset. There is no doorknob. The handle is on the inside, so the doors can't be opened from the deck entrance. You must use the security keypad. The Price family probably feels that knocking and doorbells are too middle-class.

Most of the girls at Cliffs View are intimidated by Jessa, but Bryn isn't. Their relationship is void of any petty jealousy that typically plagues teenage friendships, especially in high school. When it comes to school, Bryn is organized, always on time, and a diligent worker, but she is more of a free spirit when it comes to clothes, preferring secondhand vintage fashion over modern luxury labels. Her wardrobe consists mostly of jeans and T-shirts, with a few 1970sinspired sundresses. She always wears a pair of sandals. Bryn can't walk in heels, unlike Jessa, who has an entire closet categorized by heel type: wedge, slide, pump, and stiletto. Every drawer in Jessa's shoe closet is labeled so each pair has a designated spot. Bryn has trouble remembering where she flung her flip-flops off last.

As far as makeup goes, Bryn only uses mascara and sometimes lip gloss. She lets her hair air dry and mostly wears it down or pinned back in a large clip. Both Jessa and Aly go to the hairdresser once a month for highlights. The only color change in Bryn's hair comes from the sun.

Before Bryn has a chance to get Jessa's attention and ask about the picture, Luke announces, "Alright, everyone can stop panicking. Crisis averted—your video is ready to go."

Jessa is slouching and fidgeting with her blouse. Her posture may not seem like a big deal to the untrained eye, but when you really know someone, the subtle things they do that are out of the ordinary, are a big deal.

Bryn turns her attention back to the screen just as the Varsity Cheerleading Squad appears. In the video, the girls run out on the field to perform at halftime.

"GO. FIGHT. WIN! SAY IT AGAIN! GO. FIGHT. WIN!"

The camera follows Aly and Jessa as they ascend in the air for matching basket tosses, one of the most dangerous cheer stunts of all. The girls are tossed about six to eight feet, do a synchronized toe touch at the highest point, and then land safely in the arms of their bottom bases.

"TOUCHDOWN! MOVE IT IN. LET'S SCORE. ONE MORE!"

Whenever Bryn watches them, she is adamant in her belief that the cheerleaders put themselves at a higher risk of injury than the football players. The flyers must be fearless and make sure every move, each foot placement, is in the right spot. Then, they must rely on their squad to catch them. If something feels off, even slightly, the stunt is doomed. There is no turning back when you are in midair and if one of your teammates makes a mistake, you may just hit the ground hard. Bryn assumes the adrenaline rush they get after a perfect execution makes them forget about the risk of a dangerous drop. Bryn's never been interested in joining the squad she's happy to watch from the stands.

Aly's big brown eyes grow wider as she watches herself fly in the air. She reaches over to tap Jessa on the shoulder. "Did you see how high we were?" Aly says loudly so the whole class pays attention. "We hit it on point!"

Jessa smiles, and color starts to come back to her face. She sits up straight and lets out an audible exhale as if she has been holding her breath. "We do look pretty good out there," she says confidently.

Bryn gets a sense that things are back to normal as they watch more of the video. She is looking at

Jessa when she hears Brad yell over to her, "Hey Bryn, look—they captured your big solo!"

Bryn whips her head back to face the screen and sees herself on camera.

Jessa is quick to come to Bryn's defense and teases Brad. "You wish you could sing like her—that voice is going to make her millions, while you're trying to get a job coaching Junior Varsity football."

Brad puts his hands up, motioning a surrender.

The camera zooms in on Bryn the day of the Cliffs View Charity Talent Show. She is onstage sitting on a bar stool, wearing a long mint-green dress that hits right above her ankles. Bryn rarely wears jewelry, but that night she'd put on the abalone shell necklace her aunt gave her. The long necklace catches the reflection of the stage lights, illuminating Bryn's olive skin.

She has been singing and playing the guitar since she was six years old. While other little girls had their hands in glitter and markers, her fingertips were callused, like sandpaper, from strumming her acoustic guitar. Bryn played a song over and over until she got it perfect and then performed for her family. Every Friday night they had a mini concert. Her parents even blocked off a little section of the living room and set up chairs, with "reserved" signs written in bold red ink: "VIP Area." Their kitchen became a concession stand with popcorn and treats before the show.

When Bryn got a little older and girls her age were getting manicures, she kept her nails short, filed down to the skin. It didn't look pretty but was better for fretting.

Bryn doesn't like to sing in front of an audience, but the talent show was for charity, and she was in a new town, at a new school, so she promised herself she would get out of her comfort zone.

But performing in front of a crowd was not the same as performing in her living room as a child. While she was backstage waiting, she remembers feeling light-headed, her hands sweaty and her heart pounding in her chest. When the emcee first called her name, she couldn't move; it was as if her feet had grown roots into the floorboards beneath her. She doesn't even remember how she made it out to the stage. But she did make it. The evidence is right in front of her as she watches herself sing. Feeling a surge of embarrassment, Bryn lifts her hands to cover her face so that she is just peeking through her fingers. To this day, her palms still feel rough. Aly and Jessa are quick to put a stop to her modesty as they pull her hands away from her face. "Bryn, seriously, you have to watch this—you are amazing," Jessa says.

Aly chimes in. "I'm going to find a singing show for you to try out for this summer. That is what you have to do to be discovered these days."

Bryn laughs. The last thing she wants is to be discovered. The music starts to slow down, and her voice is being used as a background audio track as more pictures of classmates blanket the screen. Then, it happens so quickly, but slowly enough for Bryn to take notice. The next picture that appears is one of her, from years ago, before she came to Cliffs View. The image is black-and-white, and the edges are ripped—it's eerie and out of place, just like Jessa's picture. Then, as if it is being burned, the photo turns to an image of fiery ash. What follows is a sound that no one can ignore, a bloodcurdling scream that causes everyone in the class to cover their ears and startles Mr. Turner out of his sound sleep. He jumps up, grabs his briefcase, and storms out. "I'm too old for this," he says. "I'm done!"

The students are shouting, "Turn it off!" Luke shuts down the television, but the scream just gets louder. It's now coming from the school speakers. He walks outside and then back into the classroom. Luke's hands are clenched into tight fists. Bryn's never seen him get this angry. He yells so they can hear him over the scream. "We cancel your 'ditch day' and this is how you retaliate?" He looks at Jessa and Aly. "You two come in here, make a scene, dressed for a funeral, and whine about your 'dead' party. So, what are you you trying to pull now?"

Jessa gets defensive. "We didn't do this!" Then the scream comes to a sudden stop.

Bryn immediately grabs Jessa's hand and stares intently at her best friend. Her voice is broken and shaky. "How did *that* picture end up in the video? Something isn't right."

Jessa dips her head, averting her eyes, but finally speaks. "Bryn, I need to tell you a secret."

CHAPTER 2

LAST DAY OF SCHOOL, BREAK

*A*ly hears her friends whispering and pops her head up. With her large, dark brown eyes, pointy nose, and petite frame, she resembles one of those curious little meerkats at the zoo, peeking out of its hole. She hates being left out or feeling like a third wheel, which can happen with three close friends. The bell rings and everyone makes their way to the door. Aly pushes her way past the stampede and stops in between Bryn and Jessa. She stands on her tiptoes and arches her neck, trying to gain a couple of inches to meet them at eye level.

"Well, that was weird, what was up with those those pictures? Bryn, was that last one of you?"

Bryn nods her head.

Aly appears to be slightly disappointed, probably because she was excluded from the creepy black-and-white picture sequence.

A few months ago, Bryn and Jessa caught the flu

and had to stay home from school for a couple of days. Supposedly, Aly came over to see Jessa and just bring her homework…but she got sick the next day, so she had to stay home too. It seemed very suspicious. Bryn pictured her secretly sipping from Jessa's cup of orange juice, trying to catch the germs. Aly also refuses to sit in the backseat of Jessa's car, almost marking her territory as top best friend, which entitles her to permanent "shotgun." Bryn couldn't care less; she knows the backseat is safer and Jessa isn't the most cautious driver.

Aly starts to get anxious and twists her ponytail between her fingers. "And then that scream, Luke was totally freaking out," she says.

"We don't need a replay, Aly, we were all there," Jessa says. It's clear she's getting frustrated.

"Okay, so, who could have those pictures and why are they in the video yearbook? " Aly asks. "Hmm, oh, of course… Luke was hinting at it. I've got it—this must be a senior prank. Yes, that's definitely it," she says.

Aly does this a lot. She asks a question and then offers her own answer.

"I mean it's weird, but it's probably some of the guys playing a prank on us." she says.

"A *prank?*" Bryn asks. "I don't see how those pictures are funny. Or how a strange scream coming from the speakers is supposed to be a joke."

Jessa hops onboard with Aly's explanation."Bryn, it could totally be a senior prank!"

Aly nods her head and further explains. "Jessa,

remember when Clay Harris and Brad Beckett snuck into my window during football tryouts? Part of their Varsity initiation was to try and steal something from our slumber party. We woke up and they were going through our stuff. I bet they found a lot of random pictures and snuck some in from when we were younger as a prank, and..."

Jessa interrupts her. "Maybe they got the one of you with that awful headgear you wore at night freshman year."

Aly shrieks. "Jess! Shut up!"

Jessa smiles and touches Aly's face.

"But look how pretty you are now. C'mon, show me your smile." Aly gives her an obnoxious grin. "Cheese!"

They're starting to gloss over the facts, but something doesn't feel right. Bryn tries to keep them on track.

"That doesn't explain the...the picture of me. How did they get it? You guys, what secret are you talking about? What is so creepy about your picture, Jessa? I mean...you looked like you had seen a ghost when that picture flashed on the video."

Jessa instinctively gets her compact, carefully examining her complexion, making sure it's back to normal. As she closes it shut with a satisfied smile, she turns to Bryn to assure her everything will be fine. Maybe she's not ready to share her secret, Bryn thinks.

"Bryn, it's something that happened years ago. I

promise we will sit down later and tell you everything."

Aly pops her head up again between them. "Everything?"

Jessa ignores the question. "Aly's right—I'm sure the picture thing is just a prank and the two have nothing to do with each other, it's just a coincidence."

Bryn has an eerie feeling as they walk down the hall and head to Spanish class. The warmth from the late-season Santa Ana is gone, replaced by a chill in the air.

Aly and Jessa may have a secret. But what they don't know is that Bryn has a secret too.

CHAPTER 3

LAST DAY OF SCHOOL, SECOND
PERIOD, SPANISH CLASS

*B*ryn, Aly, and Jessa stop by their lockers as Brad and Clay walk toward them. Aly decides this is the time to bring up the pictures. "Very funny, guys, nice 'picture prank,' but we are so on to you!"

Brad motions to his lap. "How about you get on to this!" Then, he notices Bryn behind Aly. "Oh hey, Bryn, didn't see you there."

Bryn looks up and smiles, but she's still fixating on the holes in Aly's prank theory.

Aly makes her way closer to Brad. "Nice offer, Brad, but no thanks—been there, done that...and should we expect any more tricks from your crew today?"

A look of confusion sweeps across his face...but he always tends to have that look, so it really doesn't reveal much. Brad isn't Bryn's type. He's cute, in a conventional high school football player way, and she did have a moment or two over the past year with Brad…but it never really got past the occasional flirtation at a party, or a group going to the movies together. But it's obvious he is into her.

Meanwhile, Clay is oblivious to their conversation. He is checking himself out in the mirror as he spikes up his jet-black hair. He claims the mirror was already in his locker when it was assigned to him and he wasn't able to remove it.

Aly sweeps her hand over the top of his sticky gelled do. "You missed a spot," she laughs.

"Oh C'mon," Clay says. "Now, I got to fix it again!"

"Sorry," Aly says and runs to catch up with Jessa. "Did you see Brad's face? They totally did it!"

Jessa shrugs her shoulders. "I guess."

Aly starts rifling through her purse. "Where is my lipstick?" Aly's entire arm is enveloped in the abyss of her bag as she digs around. "Ah, here it is." She twists the body of the tube, examining the shade, makes a weird face, then tosses it back into the bottomless pit of her purse. "I'm going to stop in the bathroom for a minute." Her statement is more of a question, like she's asking Jessa's permission to pee.

"Just go quick," Jessa says. "I want to interrogate those guys, to make sure it's them." Jessa looks over Bryn's shoulder at Brad and Clay. "I am just not so sure, you know?"

Bryn can tell Jessa is on the fence. "I think you're right, there must be more to it." Everyone files into Ms. Día's Spanish class.

"Hola. ¿Como estás, estudiantes? La graduación es hoy, correcto?"

The students are silent as Aly and Clay sneak in after the bell.

Ms. Día places her hands on her wide hips. Their Spanish teacher always wears bright floral pencil skirts. Today her skirt is red, with a blend of yellow tulips and bright orange poppies spinning in a dizzy pattern from top to bottom. Her shoes are thin ballet style flats, and her feet are stuffed into them so tightly, each time she takes a step it looks like the material will burst. They aren't doing her figure any favors; she is barely five feet tall; a looser skirt and heels would work wonders. Ms. Día reluctantly speaks in English. "I am not playing the video until someone answers."

In a monotone voice, the class mumbles, "No, graduación es mañana."

"Ahh, muy bien, estudiantes. ¿Estás emocionado por las vacaciones de verano?"

The students look at each other. "Huh, what did she say?"

Ms. Día's hands fly up from her hips, motioning an "I give up" gesture. She pushes play and takes a seat behind her desk.

This portion of the video is different from the clip last period. The pictures are out of focus and shaky. The footage looks damaged and the background music sounds like it's from a horror movie. It begins at low volume and then slightly shifts an octave to build suspense. Then, what looks like bloody letters flash in a random formation around the screen. Whispers become background noise throughout the class:

"Cool, it's different, like a Quentin Tarantino movie."

"Creepy, this is weird."

"Is there something wrong with the TV? It's giving me a headache..."

Then another picture appears. It's the bottom of a quarry or some sort of rocky beach with a chalk outline meant to represent a dead body. The scattered bloody letters start to spell words onscreen:

D-O-U-B-L-E D-A-R-E

Ms. Día takes off her glasses and begins rubbing her eyes. *"¿Qué es esto?"* she says to herself. "I don't understand your generation's expression of art," she adds, burying her face in a magazine.

After about a minute, comforting colors return to the screen and scenes from around the campus start playing. The whispers start again. *"Looks like the editing class was trying to get creative." "I guess it will make more sense when we see it all together."*

Bryn looks back at Aly, who is frantically searching through her bag again. Then she dumps the contents of her purse on her desk. A mess of clutter tumbles out and falls onto the floor. She doesn't seem to care and continues rummaging through the items.

Aly keeps repeating, "Where is it?"

Bryn and Jessa walk over to her desk. "What are you looking for?"

Aly is now down on her hands and knees,

searching the ground. "This! Look! I've never seen this before." She picks up the lipstick from the ground, the one from earlier.

Jessa isn't impressed. "Who cares about lipstick right now. Something really weird is going on!"

Aly turns the lipstick upside down and shoves it in her friend's face. "Look at the name!"

Both Bryn and Jessa gasp as they read the name on the bottom: DOUBLE DARE. It doesn't help that the shade is a deep blood red.

Ms. Día stands up and slams her magazine on the desk like she's swatting a fly. "Sit down, ladies—back to your seats."

Aly ignores the instructions and turns toward Brad. She starts swinging the lipstick in the air.

"Did you do this, like some sort of sick joke?"

Brad looks more confused than normal. "Jesus, Al, you're losing it! I have no idea what you are talking about." He looks back at Clay, who sits behind him and makes a "cuckoo, cuckoo" twirl with his hand.

Aly isn't backing off. "I'm not crazy, you know, we talked about this homecoming night…about…"

Jessa pushes Aly down in her seat. "Aly, sit down —you don't want to get in trouble, not today."

Aly obeys and Jessa whispers in her ear. Bryn can barely make out what she's saying. "What did you tell him on homecoming? We swore we'd never…Does he know about…her, that night—?"

Aly faces Jessa, with her most apologetic expression.

"I'm sorry... He just knows a little, it came up, we had a lot to drink and were at the cliffs—you know, the same spot. But I didn't...I hardly said anything."

Jessa shakes her head in disbelief. "I find that hard to believe considering what we just saw." She points dramatically at the TV. "And this!" she says as she grabs the lipstick back.

Aly looks like she is about to cry. "I screwed up, but I promise I didn't say anything that would come ba—"

Jessa tightly grips the lipstick and puts her other hand up to Aly's face. "Just stop talking—you've said enough."

Ms. Día stomps her fat little sausage foot. "Silencio! Do I need to send you to the principal?"

The girls shake their heads and sit quietly. The teacher lets out a deep exhale and pushes the play button. But DOUBLE DARE keeps pulsating on screen. Then you hear Aly's voice over the loudspeaker repeatedly: "Double Dare, Double Dare Double Dare..."

Aly looks back at Brad. "I swear, Brad, stop this..."

Jessa goes up and turns off the video. "Sorry, Ms. Día, but all this is very triggering for Aly." Jessa walks close to the teacher. "She has mental episodes, bad panic attacks—it runs in her family."

Ms. Dia pulls the plug that connects the loud speaker to the classroom. "Bastante! Enough."

Aly slumps in her chair and looks at Bryn. "I don't think these are pranks," she says.

Bryn nods in agreement. "Me either."

They all remain silent until the bell rings. Jessa leaves the class first and waits in the hallway for Bryn and Aly. As soon as the other students clear out of the way, she tells them her plan. "We need to find out who is doing this now and put a stop to it. I refuse to start the summer off this way. First, the party is cancelled, and now we have to spend the day tracking down some loser trying to scare us with pictures and what, creepy voices that are supposed to sound like us?"

Bryn huffs. "*Sound* like us? That was clearly Aly's voice."

"Aly, go talk to Clay and find out if Brad said anything to him, and seriously, see what he knows—don't mess this up," Jessa says.

Aly just nods, her head still down. She looks afraid to even speak to Jessa after her secret slip-up during Spanish class.

Jessa turns to Bryn and firmly grips her shoulders. "You go back to Luke's class and get him to give you that flash drive, the one that the whole video yearbook is on."

"Get the flash drive? Why would he give it to me?"

Aly and Jessa both smirk. Jessa loosens her grip and steps back. "I see the way he looks at you," she says.

Aly nods. "Yeah, he totally has a crush on you."

Bryn can't help blushing a bit. "I have no idea what you are talking about—he's, our teacher."

Jessa doesn't seem to care about Bryn's excuse. "Bryn, just tell him you want to watch yourself singing…how you were so embarrassed when it first played and didn't get a chance to watch, and when he's not looking, slip it in your bag and walk out. Let's meet here in one hour." Jessa claps her hands together, sealing the game plan. No going back.

As Bryn begins her mission to get a copy of the video yearbook, she thinks about how determined she was to get into Cliffs View High in the first place. The sacrifices she made to get here. Now, so close to completing the year, Bryn is nervous that everything she's worked for could fall apart.

CHAPTER 4

ONE YEAR EARLIER, CRESCENT PINE, NORTHERN CALIFORNIA

Bryn has enough credits to graduate, so she takes what they call a "study period" in the middle of the day and basically has an hour of free time. Her initial plan was to go for a run to clear her head, but now she is walking back to Luke's class to try to see if she can get an early copy of the video yearbook.

While walking toward Luke's classroom, Bryn thinks about where she was last year, before coming to Cliff's View.

ONE YEAR EARLIER, Crescent Pine, California

Bryn's hometown, Crescent Pine, was about thirty miles inland from Santa Barbara. The local high school in Bryn's district was Crescent Pine High School. From the name, it sounds like the school was nestled in nature, with beautiful trees and fresh clean air flowing through the classrooms. A couple years ago, this would have been an accurate description. But two things changed the landscape of a once prosperous area: a devastating drought and the closure of the Olson Textile Factory. California was in one of the state's worst droughts resulting in crushing agricultural and financial losses. The surrounding nature was desperate for water, and most of the trees were dry and bare.

The shut-down factory left the town dry in a different way. Once the main source of income for the folks of Crescent County, now was a dilapidated reminder of the city's high unemployment rate. The homeless and the high school dropouts used the abandoned factory as a hangout, a skate park, and a place to drink and do drugs. The people there, including the police, just ignored it, which made the problem worse. Bryn spent part of her junior year at Crescent Pine High. It wasn't working out so she was homeschooled for the last semester.

This year she decided to live with her aunt three hundred miles away and go to high school in the city of Cliffs View in Southern California for her senior year. The high schools in the Cliffs View area had a variety of Advanced Placement classes, college prep courses, and opportunities for scholarship programs. In other words, they had money, the type of funding that Crescent Pine didn't. At the time, her parents were separating, and Bryn's mother saw the move as a great opportunity for her daughter, as she too was looking for her own way out. It was clear for a while how disconnected their family had become. They were all yearning for change and willing to take risks to make it happen.

Unfortunately, Bryn's father chose his own escape method: after losing his job he decided to give up on pretty much everything else. The last time she spoke with him was the morning she left, more than a year ago.

She replays that morning often, wishing there was something more they could have said to each other, but mainly she wonders if her father even thinks twice about it. Everything changed then, and Bryn remembers how it played out:

Bryn set the alarm, checking it multiple times before she went to bed. The next day was her chance at a fresh start, going to a high school in a new city. She needed to be up at 5:15 a.m. to catch the train to Aunt Rae's and wasn't risking any chance of missing it. Like most mornings, the alarm clock served as a backup, because her father's hacking cough at 5 a.m. woke everyone up. She heard it right on schedule, along with her mom yelling, then crying; this was also common in their home. As Bryn walked into the kitchen, her mother wiped her face and quickly retreated into the bathroom. That's how their days started. Dad became a smoker again a couple years ago, after almost fifteen nicotine-free years . The constant coughing accompanied the disgusting habit. Bryn chose not to mention the smoking anymore; it was the least of his problems and would only start a fight. He didn't even look up as she walked to the fridge, grabbed the carton of orange juice, and said good morning to her father. He just sat there, holding that cigarette in a shaky hand, barely able to keep it steady as he inhaled. Her dad glared at an empty bottle of whiskey next to the dirty tin can he used as an ashtray. Bryn couldn't decide whether he was angry at the bottle for what it had done to his life, specifically his marriage, or just mad that there was no more whiskey. Bryn figured it was the latter.

Her mom walked back in the kitchen and hugged her daughter before starting some coffee. "Big day, Brynny! It's the first day of the rest of your life."

Bryn smirked at the cliché. Lately it had been hard for her mother to come up with inspiring words of her own, so she perpetually plagiarized quotes from her inspirational self-help books. Bryn didn't point it out. She just kissed her mom and told her how much she would miss her.

"Oh Bryn, you just loved spending summers with Aunt Rae—you never wanted to come home. Just think of this as an extended summer trip, but school is top priority—keep your grades up and get that college scholarship, hon'."

"I know, mama, that's the plan," said Bryn.

"You two will have so much fun; you're more like…sisters."

Bryn felt the tears well up in her eyes and she hugged her mom tight. Rae was her mother's younger sister, and they were fourteen years apart, which made Aunt Rae and Bryn only seven years apart.

Her dad let out another violent, startling cough, causing her mom to spill coffee on the counter.

"Jesus, Susan! Clean that up right away, or it'll stain!" He knew how to break up a nice mother–daughter moment. Bryn's mother grabbed a sponge and just did what he said. Bryn could hardly stand to be in the same room with him. She looked at her mother and at that moment, realized they both felt the same way. Susan Matthews-Powell was smart and beautiful, but the last couple of years had really taken a toll on her. Her eyes, once a bright ocean blue, were now polluted with a bloodshot haze. A sign of too little sleep and too many tears. She'd let her hair go gray and rarely took the time to wear makeup or "prepare for the day" like she used to. But behind the sadness, Bryn could still see a strong woman determined to get out of this rut, this routine of despair. She wanted her mother to be happy again. She deserved to be.

The years had been far worse for her father, Maxwell Powell, because of the heavy drinking and smoking. Bryn hated seeing this drunk version of him all the time. He was unpredictable; at one moment talkative and happy, then seconds later angry at everyone, incoherently blaming the world for his problems. Bryn no longer recognized her dad.

After witnessing the rapid decline of his mental and physical health, Bryn feared he was gone for good. She always used to describe her dad as strong and reliable, a man who loved his family more than anything. When she was a kid, he would lift her up onto his shoulders and tell her she deserved the best view of the world. Sitting up there, Bryn felt like anything was possible. Now, his shoulders could barely hold up his own T-shirt; they seemed to sink into the rest of his body as if the weight from the last few years was pulling him down into a permanent slump. "Dad, Dad…" Bryn said, waiting on a response.

He finally looked at her for the first time that morning.

"Dad, I'm going now."

"Uh-huh," he said.

"I love you," Bryn said. She really did love her father.

"Be safe," he said, and reached for another cigarette.

"Okay, Dad."

And that was it. Bryn's mom shook her head, and they headed out to the car.

HER MOM WAS RIGHT: summers at Aunt Rae's were the best. She lived steps to the beach in a cozy two-bedroom condo. Bryn's aunt ran every morning on the sand; she was always training for one of the many local races. Rae hung her race medals in the hallway of her home. They covered most of the wall, too many to count, and running shoes lined the garage.

Her aunt explained in a highly technical way how

you need to rotate shoes every three months when you are racking up high mileage. It was very important to prevent injuries. Rae was Pre-Law at CVU and was beyond excited to have her niece move in, saying, "Bryn, it'll be like we are college roomies!"

Rae worked at one of the coolest restaurants on the beach. She was also very dedicated to her yoga practice. Her aunt was determined to turn Bryn into a little "yogi." She said it was the best way to stay grounded when the universe tries to knock you down.

CHAPTER 5

LAST DAY OF SCHOOL, STUDY PERIOD

*B*ryn gets a whiff of a familiar scent—cologne—and hears footsteps behind her. The fragrance brings her back to the present. It's funny how your sense of smell conjures up specific memories. She knows Brad wears that cologne, or maybe it's aftershave. It smells rustic, but with a tad of sweetness like vanilla. The type of cologne you'd see in a commercial where the guy just walks into a cozy cabin, carrying wood for the fire, but for some reason he is wearing a leather jacket and torn jeans, without a shirt.

Brad doesn't wear a leather jacket, but she can see him buying into the concept of a commercial like that enough to shell out $80 for a designer cologne.

He didn't overdo it with the fragrance today. She imagines him applying just a drop behind the ear or the nape of his tan neck. The aroma intertwines with the afternoon breeze swiftly making its way to

Bryn's nose. It really makes it impossible for him to sneak up on her.

"Hey Bryn, do you have a few minutes to talk?" Brad has a study period too, but he usually spends it in the gym.

Bryn is about to blow him off and focus on the mission at hand, but he looks concerned, even a little afraid. The vulnerability in his eyes is intriguing.

"Sure. What's up?"

Brad motions over to the benches beneath the palm trees adjacent to Luke's classroom. "How about we go sit down—it's kind of complicated." The tone of his voice sounds sincere, which is out of character for Brad.

Bryn tucks her hair behind her ear as she glances toward the benches. "Sure, but I really have to...get some stuff done before break is over," she says.

"Oh, okay, yeah, it won't take that long—I just need someone to talk to. That was so crazy in Spanish class, right?"

Bryn nods as they walk past Luke's classroom. She notices Luke sitting at the computer, but he stands up when he sees the two of them.

Brad waves and Luke walks over to the open door. "Hey, are you two done with the day already, sneaking out early?"

Bryn smiles and is quick with an explanation. "No, it's our study period, and we just have a few things to talk about before the pep rally this afternoon," she lies.

Brad puts up his hand, motioning to Luke for a high-five. "You'll be at the rally, right, Mr. H.?"

"Yes, of course, I wouldn't miss it."

Bryn and Brad continue walking as Luke stands there watching them for a minute before disappearing back into the classroom.

Brad shakes his head. "I don't know what it is about that guy."

Bryn doesn't get his comment; Luke is such a laid-back T.A. "What do you mean? The class was easy and our final project, a personal essay about anything we want—it beats that awful History class we had."

"What? Mr. Decker's history class was so awesome! We just watched movies all the time."

Brad is right. Mr. Decker just shows movies and then decides grades based on his own weird criteria. He told Bryn he gave her a B+, her only B, because he didn't like the socks, she was wearing one day. After final grades were issued a couple of days ago, Bryn left the dirty socks in his mailbox with a card that read:

Dear Mr. Decker,

> *I'm sure you can use these. They're for specific types of teachers, maybe you've heard of them:*
> *"My teaching socks."**
> *Have a great summer! —Bryn*
> **Some brands spell socks with a "u."*

"No, Luke's class was chill. But he just seems off to me, like he is trying too hard to be *cool*," says Brad.

Bryn needs more of an explanation. "I'm not following—what do you mean?"

"I don't know, it's like when I went to elementary school with this kid who was such a weirdo, but then by middle school he had made new friends, started getting into sports, and by high school you'd never know he was a former loser," Brad says.

"Maybe that is just your perception of him…and that kid was always cool," Bryn says.

"Heh, I don't think so. You could tell he was still holding a grudge and inside still that chubby kid with a bad haircut."

Bryn stops walking for a second. "And you get that feeling about Luke?"

"Not exactly, says Brad. But yeah… It's like he's trying too hard, and what is with his weird fascination with astrology? Aren't horoscopes and shit more of a girl thing?"

Bryn snickers. "You mean astronomy?" Luke has photos displayed on his desk of different constellations and planets, not typical for an English T.A. "I don't know, it's a hobby for him. I think it's interesting to look at the world beyond our planet, like even if you can't see it, there is something bigger out there."

Brad scratches his head. "Yeah, well, all that is a little too 'sci-fi nerd' for me."

Bryn decides she has had enough with Brad's arrogant assumptions and changes the subject as they sit on the bench underneath the palm trees. "What did you want to talk to me about? You mentioned that picture from the video."

"Yea—you know, the one that flashed onscreen and then Aly went all psycho on me," Brad says.

"Uh-huh…What about it?" Bryn asks. "Did you have something to do with it?"

"No way!" But it's weird. Do you remember after we left the homecoming dance and we all went to hang out at the cliffs? I may have had a few beers, and Aly too, but—"

Bryn interrupts him. "I remember there was a lot of partying and Aly had way too much to drink, right?"

"Yea, so Aly told me a story about a girl, an accident…before junior year. I didn't think much of it then, but when I saw the picture in the video, and the words on the screen that said: 'Double Dare,' it clicked."

"What clicked?" Bryn asks.

"That night, when I said we should play a game— Aly totally freaked out, almost hyperventilated even. She did the same thing in class today."

Bryn remembers Aly's panic attack and the game Brad suggested on Homecoming night. "You wanted to play Truth or Dare?"

CHAPTER 6

HOMECOMING NIGHT, OCTOBER 28TH, EIGHT MONTH'S EARLIER, AUNT RAE'S CONDO

*B*ryn stared at the makeup bag that she kept in the small bathroom cabinet. She had concealer, mascara, and a sheer berry lip gloss; that's it. Jessa and Aly had a full day of homecoming dance prep, which included hair salon, tanning, and makeup appointments. Bryn was doing her own hair and makeup and planned to meet up with them later. Bryn had never been excited about dances, and hundreds of excuses to cancel were racing through her head. Food poisoning—that's always a good one; all you had to say is you can't be far from the bathroom, and no one asked questions.

But then, she glanced over at her homecoming dress hanging right under the open window. It swayed back and forth as if taunting her with its own dance, and the breeze whispered *"Wear me, wear me..."*

Last week at a small boutique near Jessa's house, the three girls went shopping. Bryn had no intention of buying a dress but was happy to go along and help her friends decide between their top choices. Jessa and Aly had three dresses each on hold.

While they were in the dressing room, Bryn began browsing toward the back of the store and a dress caught her eye. From the front it looked like a classic Little Black Dress, but as she got closer, she could see the intricate lace design traveling all the way down to the bottom, which on Bryn would hit about mid-thigh. The straps were matching lace and when she held the dress out in front of her, she noticed it was backless. Bryn had never worn a dress like that, and she pictured putting her long hair up, to expose her bare back. As she looked at it in the light, she saw that the material was not just black lace but had specks of gold throughout. Bryn didn't identify herself as the "fashion maven" that Jessa and Aly claimed to be, but she did appreciate a timeless dress like this. A dress that may look simple and sweet from the front but as she inspected it closer, there were so many beautiful details, it was mesmerizing. Then, when she spun around and revealed the sexy open back, any first impressions about the dress or the girl wearing it could be questioned. Plus, Rae had a pair of gold heels that fit Bryn perfectly. The shoes were only a couple of inches high, so she'd be able to walk in them...maybe.

As Bryn continued to inspect the dress, her vision was momentarily impaired by an explosion of bright pink. Aly came out of the dressing room in a skintight strapless dress. She looked like "Bubble Gum Barbie!" Which was kind of perfect for Aly.

Aly stood in front of the three-way mirror that gave her a view from every angle. Bryn walked over and helped her fasten the zipper, then noticed Aly was an inch taller than her. Bryn looked down and saw the high heels in a matching bright pink. Aly smiled and kicked up her foot.

"They're almost five inches, I love them… Do you think it's too much pink?"

Bryn smiled. "Aly, for you, it is just the right amount of pink—you pull it off."

Aly was adjusting the dress and sucking in her stomach. "No carbs until after homecoming. But I think this is the one. Oh, and Brad can wear a bright pink tie, to match!"

Aly asked Brad to homecoming during the summer. She wanted to secure a date and not have to worry about it, but they weren't an official couple.

Bryn and Jessa were not bringing dates to the dance. It did not start out that way.

Jessa was "off and on again" dating Conner Kenneth Richardson III. Some of the guys called him "CK-3." Jessa used his full name when she introduced him to people. Bryn could tell it made Jessa feel like she was dating royalty or something. But Conner was far from Prince Charming. Jessa and Conner were supposed to go to the dance together, but the week before Homecoming Conner got busted on school surveillance sneaking into the campus pool. He wasn't alone. He was with Michelle Lewis,

"Shelly," a sophomore. They apparently also forgot their swimsuits. So, he was banned from all activity's homecoming weekend. Jessa was mortified when she found out and told Bryn and Aly all about it,

'Ugh, skinny-dipping with a sophomore! What was he thinking? And of course, it's with Slutty Shelly! They can have each other.' Jessa cut Connor out of the group after the cheating scandal.

The dance was three days later; everyone already had dates. Jessa could bring a guy from another school, she knew plenty, but at this point it was about principle she said, *'No more guys; we're going solo, Bryn.'* Suddenly Bryn was part of Jessa's "Single Lady" movement. Bryn had not been planning to go to the dance.

The truth is, Brad had confessed his feelings for Bryn a few weeks prior and really wanted her to be his date and break it off with Aly. Bryn was not looking to get involved in some sort of love triangle or hurt a friend and she decided it would be best to sit this one out. But after the skinny-dip scandal, Jessa convinced Bryn to go with her.

* * *

WHEN BRYN TRIED on the black dress, it fit perfectly; no alterations or dieting needed. She had to buy it. But looking at the dress in her bathroom, Bryn realized she needed the hair and makeup to go with it. There was only one person she trusted with this: Aunt Rae. Bryn walked downstairs and saw her aunt in the kitchen. She wore headphones and danced around the table as she threw veggies into the blender: kale, spinach, and some weird purple root that looked like it was from another planet. Bryn could tell Rae just came back from a run, because of her bright white and orange Nike shoes, running shorts, and orange sports bra with a white swoosh that matched her shoes. That was not by accident. She could be on the cover of "Marathon Monthly."

Rae was beautiful, and people told Bryn they look alike. Bryn saw some similarities: the same long, wavy honey-colored hair, but different eyes. Rae's eyes were exquisite; only one other person in the Matthews family had them. They took on different colors, so sometimes they resembled hazel like Bryn's. But Bryn had seen them change from blue to jade green and even yellow.

Aunt Rae spun around to start the blender, and saw Bryn. She pulled down her headphones. "Did you come down to have a yummy glass of green goddess juice? I know you did!"

Bryn peeked at the brownish-green concoction as she walked to the fridge.

"I think I'll pass." Bryn grabbed a bottle of water. "But I do need a little blending help of my own." She motioned to her face and hair.

Rae's eyes literally changed color with excitement. "Yay! Bryn, I've been wanting to do your hair and makeup since you got here. You are such a natural beauty, but this is a special occasion, and a dramatic smokey eye will look perfect with that dress."

Suddenly Bryn pictured raccoon-like eyes and felt like this was a bad idea. "What is a 'smokey eye?'" she asked.

"Don't worry, it will look classy—you don't need a lot of makeup, trust me."

Bryn nodded. "Okay." She liked seeing her aunt happy. "Of course, I trust you."

Rae reached over and started playing with Bryn's hair. "We'll sweep your hair up into a loose bun, add a little volume to the top, and enhance those natural curls."

Bryn smiled. "Sounds great."

"When you were little, I tried to put matching clips in your hair… You pulled them right out. Well, you never were the girly one." Rae's voice begins to crack a bit. "Sorry, I get emotional; it's just…"

Bryn interrupts. "It's okay, but we really need to get started. I'm meeting at Jessa's for pictures in an hour."

Rae nodded and headed to her room. "I'll grab my makeup."

Bryn washed her face, tied her hair back, and put on her robe. She looked in the mirror and then again at her dress, realizing there was still a lot to be done and not a lot of time.

* * *

BRYN'S CHEEKS ached from smiling so much since arriving at Jessa's house for the pre-party. She didn't understand why they needed to take so many pictures before the dance. There was already a photographer hired to take pictures at the dance. The homecoming photo session started in Jessa's front yard with "Girl Pictures." Of course, the professional photographer, had a list that Jessa created to ensure he got all the right poses. She insisted on a variety of angles and her own version of candid shots. Jessa didn't like to be caught off guard for pictures. For her, "the worst thing ever" is a picture with her mouth open or laughing from that bad angle that makes you look like you have three chins. So, they took "posed candid's:" the three girls laughing (with heads correctly positioned), hugging, and pretending to eat appetizers.

After the photo shoot, it was time for a break before the guys showed up. Bryn was excited to eat some of the food that had so far just been used as props. The chicken skewers tasted great, and the cheese platter smelled of basil, garlic, and fresh gouda. At least the food was real...but everything else felt fake. Jessa and Aly headed over to examine the pictures and delete the unflattering ones. Bryn saw the black stretch limo slowly pulling up the private driveway. Clay had his upper body out of the sunroof.

"Who's ready to PAR-TAY!!?" He was only wearing a black bow tie, no shirt. "Woo-hoo!! You know I am!" Clay started beating on his chest with his fists, gorilla style.

Bryn assumed the pre-party festivities had already started in the limo.

The photographer snapped more photos. Clay disappeared back into the limo. But the show wasn't over…this time the side window rolled down and sticking out of it was a bare butt.

Bryn laughed, while Aly looked shocked. It was obvious to her that was Brad's butt. She tried to save face.

Aly whistled and said, "Well, that's my boyfriend…always making an entrance."

The photographer took photos as Clay put his head right next to Brad's butt and howled like a wolf. "There is a full moon tonight!"

Jessa stood in front of the photographer and swung her hands in the air. "No, no, no pictures of this, please!" She yelled at the guys in the limo. "You better have your suits on when you come out—I'm serious. No one wants to see that!"

The limo parked in front of Jessa's deck. Clay came out with his date, Amelia, who went to a different school. Amelia pawed at Clay's chest as he buttoned up his dress shirt. "Oh Jessa, lighten up. He looks so good without his shirt and just that cute bow tie, like those dancers…in Vegas. I think they're Swedish or something."

Jessa didn't care for Amelia. "It's the 'Down Under' show in Vegas and it started in Australia."

Jessa knew her sexy stripper stats. Amelia rolled her eyes and turned her attention back to Clay.

Brad walked up behind them and apologetically greeted Jessa. "Didn't mean to make you upset—just trying to have a little fun."

"Well, I'm glad you found your pants," Jessa said.

Brad carried three separate corsages. He handed the first one to Jessa. It had a yellow rose in the center surrounded by daises. Bryn and Aly stood next to each other, and Bryn held her breath as he passed Aly and handed Bryn a corsage full of red roses with a gold ribbon. Finally, he handed *his date* Aly her flowers. Aly's corsage had a combination of pink carnations and pink roses. There was an awkward silence that lasted way too long. In class, they learned about the history of corsages. In the seventeenth century they were used to ward off evil spirits; *corsage* comes from the Latin word *corpus*, or *body*. Over time, corsages garnered a new meaning, less eerie, but the type of flowers you gave someone revealed specific feelings or intentions. Pink and yellow roses were for friendship. Red roses meant passion and romance. Aly knew it, even if she doubted Brad was paying attention to the lesson that day. But Aly was quick to fix the situation in her favor.

"Brad definitely took my advice," she says, smiling at Bryn and Jessa. "I told him red would go perfect with your dress, Bryn, and of course I wanted pink, and yellow complements Jessa's blue dress. We thought you two should have corsages even if you don't have dates."

Jessa whipped her head toward Aly. "First off, we are *choosing* not to go to the dance strapped to the arm of a man," she says. "We are strong, independent women."

Jessa's feminist rant took a backslide as she shifted the focus to fashion and modeled her head-to-toe ensemble. "Second, for the record, the correct color of my dress is aquamarine, just like my Louboutin's." Jessa's dress was a stylish one-shoulder sheath mini, and as if it wasn't short enough, it also had a slit in the side revealing just a bit too much leg. Her shoes were red-soled Christian Louboutin stilettos. Also, a little too much for high school homecoming, with a price tag of $595...but what was the saying...*if the shoe fits.*

After what seemed like the five-hundredth picture, they all headed to the limo. Amelia walked next to Bryn. Bryn smelled tequila on her breath. Amelia De Leon went to the private Catholic girls' school just outside of Cliffs View. She had been dating Clay for a few months.

Miss Margarita grabbed Bryn's hand and stalled her for a moment. "I have to tell you something." Every one of Amelia's exhales was drenched with Jose Cuervo. "You should have heard Brad when we pulled up—his mouth literally dropped open. He kept saying, 'Damn, is that Bryn? She looks so hot.' Clay had to snap him out of it and punch him in the arm and was like, 'Umm, isn't your date Aly? Get it together, bro.'"

Bryn shook her head a bit. "I never dress up like this, so he is just surprised. I don't want to get Aly upset, okay, Amelia. Can we just not bring it up?"

Amelia held on to Bryn as she wobbled down the deck steps. "Of course, let's have fun tonight—you are my girrrrl, Bryn!"

Bryn sat on the opposite side of Brad in the limo, but she could feel him sneaking those looks. It was like he didn't care who noticed. Meanwhile, Aly was getting cozy with a bottle of champagne, downing as many glasses as possible before the limo pulled up to the CV High gymnasium.

The homecoming theme was "A Night Under the Stars." A beautiful night sky was projected all over the dome ceiling, so it resembled a planetarium. There were even constellations, comets, and shooting stars. Bryn glanced over and saw the teaching staff toward the back exit. Luke was operating the lighting equipment. He noticed Bryn and she gave him a thumbs-up and pointed up at the indoor sky he'd created. "Amazing," Bryn mouthed with an approving nod. Luke walked toward their group and accidentally tripped the projector cord. The entire gym went black.

Brad and Clay insisted on calling attention to the blunder. "Party foul!" They pointed at Luke which drew more attention.

Luke plugged the cord back in. Everything was back in its place. But the guys didn't let it go.

"What a tool—walk much?" Brad said.

Aly jumped to Luke's defense to try to make Brad jealous.

"Who cares if he's clumsy…Luke is like the hottest T.A. ever." Brad didn't hear her comment or maybe he did and just didn't care.

"Ladies, let's go dance," Aly said.

On the dance floor, the only thing Aly was missing was a stripper pole. She had a lot of champagne, but these were standard moves for Aly. Especially her signature move, which Bryn believed did have roots in exotic dancing. She slowly swayed her hips as she bent down to the ground and then arched her back as she popped back up.

Jessa noticed she was going a little too far and grabbed her arm. "Aly, you're drunk dancing, again. Get your shit together."

Aly reached for Brad. "Come dance, baby, show us your moves."

Brad, Clay, and Amelia headed over to the dance floor. Amelia's dance moves surpassed everyone's; she threw in that Latin flair and then started to grind up against Clay. Jessa watched Amelia dance. She looked jealous. Amelia and Jessa were opposites, yet strikingly similar. Like they could switch places in some parallel universe. Both were the same height and had long, thick hair, Jessa's blond, and Amelia's is black. They could both be in a Pantene hair commercial. It was obvious they spent a lot of time on their makeup and appearance. Jessa had large dark blue eyes and Amelia's were a dark brown, but both had the same almond shape that made them look like they were always up to something sneaky.

Clay and Amelia moved off to their own corner of the dance floor and would most likely be there the rest of the night until the teachers told them to cool off.

Jessa and Aly resumed center stage and Brad inched closer to Bryn, thinking he was being sly, he whispered to her: "You look great, by the way."

Bryn decided that was her cue to go get some air. "Alright ladies, I'm taking a break," she said. "I'm still getting used to these heels."

Aly laughed. "Are you kidding? You call those heels? *These* are heels!" Aly kicked up her foot to show off her five-inch stilettos, but she lost her balance and fell flat on her butt. Bryn reached down to offer her a hand, but Aly refused.

"I've got it, I've got it!" Then Aly glared at Brad and in a whiny six-year-old little-girl voice, said, "Why didn't you catch me?"

Brad just laughed. Aly stood up and put her hands on her hips. She looked at Bryn out of the corner of her eyes and said accusingly, "Maybe because you were staring at my friend?" Aly was slurring her words and was still off balance from her fall. She put her hand on Jessa's shoulder to steady herself.

"C'mon, you noticed it too, Jessa. Throw on a scandalous dress and too much makeup and what, now 'blah' Bryn is suddenly the hot one?"

Jessa grabbed Aly. "Aly, you are out of control!"

They walked toward the bathroom and Jessa mouthed back "Sorry" to Bryn.

Bryn hurried outside to escape the drama and sat on the edge of the fountain behind the gym. She slipped off her heels and stretched out her toes. She was already getting blisters.

Bryn was sitting on the fountain rim when Luke walked up behind her. She blushed when she recognized the familiar voice. "That is some dress, Miss Matthews."

Luke wore tan pants and a tucked in solid black button-down shirt. He looked very handsome and almost as uncomfortable as Bryn all dressed up.

"You clean up nicely, too," Bryn said. She felt a need to explain her extravagant dress. "I went shopping with Jessa and Aly...and they wouldn't let me leave the store without it. I guess it's not really my usual style."

Luke glanced back into the gym, then walked closer and sat next to Bryn. He looked down at the corsage on her wrist.

Bryn felt she should explain that as well. "Brad brought corsages for Jessa and me, even though we didn't have dates."

Luke had an expression more serious than usual. "Be careful around that guy...and, well, all of *them* tonight. I didn't say anything, but just a warning: the other teachers suspect drinking and are about to investigate."

Bryn was quick to defend herself. "I don't drink."

Luke nodded. "I didn't accuse you...it's just you

seem like such a part of that group now and sooner or later…" His voice trailed off a bit. "Homecoming parties can get a bit crazy and I just want you to be safe."

It was the first time all night that Bryn felt something semi-real and didn't regret going to the dance. Luke's shirt sleeves were slightly rolled up revealing his strong forearms. Bryn couldn't help her eyes trailing up to his biceps and shoulders. His muscles were visible beneath the fabric. She continued her gaze past his neck until she met him at eye-level. Bryn knew it was against the rules but decided to go for it anyway and leaned closer to Luke, slightly tilting her head to the side so their lips were mere inches apart. Just as Bryn shut her eyes, Luke jerked his body back and fell right into the fountain with a loud "Splash!"

At that moment, Bryn saw Amelia and Clay walk out the back gym door. Clay laughed and pointed at Luke. "Whoa…Teach, it looks like you need help with your balance tonight."

They were both so entertained by the fall it looked like they didn't catch Bryn almost kissing him just seconds before. Luke climbed out of the fountain while Clay was still cracking jokes.

"Or were you trying to get some change and fell in?" Clay obnoxiously reached in his pocket. "I can loan you some money, man."

Luke walked up to Clay. He towered over him. "I'm just a little exhausted from spending hours setting up the gym for your last homecoming." Luke shook the water out of his hair. Clay was standing directly in the splash zone and the fountain water hit him in the face. "Sorry about that, buddy." Luke smiled as he walked off. "Luckily, I have some gym clothes here and I am going to change. You all enjoy your evening."

Bryn worried if anyone saw, but decided to forget about what just happened between her and Luke for now. She figured if Amelia and Clay saw her trying to make a move on the T.A., they would have said something right away.

Amelia motioned over to the parked limo. "We're going to get another glass of champagne. She winked at Bryn. "You should join us."

"Luke just told me the staff suspects drinking, and if you get caught you'll be suspended." Bryn said.

"Whatever, we'll take the party to the beach," Clay said. "I'm over high school dances anyway."

Clay and Amelia went back into the gym to get the rest of their group. Clay came back with a couple more guys, Tyson Chen and Jason Berger."Ty and Jayce are joining us," he said.

"Wait, wait!" Amelia shouted as she ran out of the gym and hopped in the limo. She had two extra purses on her shoulder. "Snatch and grab, baby!"

"You're so bad," Jayce said.

"I guess the purse-check volunteer went on a break, so I grabbed a couple," Amelia said.

"Whose are those?" Bryn asks.

Amelia shrugged her shoulders. "Who cares? Let's see what we got."

Bryn knew Amelia was very wealthy and didn't need to steal purses. *Maybe she liked the thrill.* Amelia dumped the purses on the limo floor. Ty, Jayce, and Amelia rummaged through the items.

"Woo—some cash, gum, what's this—maybe something good," Amelia said as she pulled out a prescription bottle and read the label. "Ugh, it's an antibiotic, no fun."

"Someone probably needs that, Amelia," Bryn said as she grabbed the bottle to look at the name.

"Oh Bryn, you are such a goody-goody," Amelia said as she imitated proper ladylike posture.

"Just saying, I think they have cameras in the gym now," Bryn added.

"Whatever—not my school, not my problem." Amelia put the cash in her cleavage and tossed the rest of the stuff in the back. Bryn made a note to grab that prescription bottle and bring it back to the school.

* * *

THE DRIVER PARKED the limo in the parking lot adjacent to the cliffs. Clay and Brad ignored the "Do Not Enter" signs, and walked over to a part of the cliffs that had beach access. There was a rope they'd used before, to climb down to the shore.

Aly grabbed two plastic cups and the last bottle of champagne. She handed a cup to Bryn. "I'm so sorry about before, I don't know what came over me... I know you are not into Brad and...well, I think it's awesome you went all out for homecoming even if you don't have a guy to go with…"

Bryn felt Aly's attempt at an apology was passive-aggressive but decided it was best to move on.

Aly poured champagne in both cups.

Bryn figured a few sips won't hurt. "Cheers, Aly, it's all good."

Aly hugged her a little too hard. "I love you, Brynny!"

Clay and Brad came back up from the rocks. Brad shook his head. "It's a no-go—a part of the cliff may have fallen because a big-ass boulder is blocking the main entrance and the rope we use is gone, so there is no way to climb down."

Clay was determined to keep the party going. "Let's go to the lookout spot!"

Aly dropped her cup and shrieked, "No F-in' way!"

Jessa snapped at Aly. "How many times do I have to tell you to chill out tonight?"

Aly did not seem chill. "Jess, I'm not going back there…"

Jessa whispered in Aly's ear, "Fine, we will have the limo take you home and I'm sure Brad won't mind spending some quality time with Bryn tonight."

Aly picked up her cup and salvaged the last sip of champagne. She realized it was best to stick around. She ran ahead to catch up with Brad, calling, "Hey, wait for me—these shoes aren't designed for a cliff run."

The lookout was a short walk after the second

parking lot on Ocean Drive. The erosion of the sea wall damaged most of the cliff's access routes, but there was still a place, nestled within the bluffs, perfect for an intimate get-together. The lack of streetlights kept the group concealed, but also made it hard to see the dangerous drop-offs along the edge. Even with a prominent sign that screamed UNSTABLE CLIFFS, with bright yellow letters, beachgoers unfamiliar with the terrain took chances, and lifeguards were called out often for rescues.

Ty and Jayce stood back by the limo. Bryn saw clouds of smoke waft through the air. The pungent smell lured Amelia out. "You two better share," she said. Jayce passed her the joint. Amelia put it up to her glossy red lips and inhaled. She blew perfect circle-shaped smoke rings. "Ooooh, I'm going to hold on to this." Amelia flashed a smile and took off running toward the rest of the group. Ty and Jayce playfully chased after her. "Hey, Amelia, pass it back —I bet it tastes better after your mouth has been on it," Ty said.

They joined the others and sat on the rocks; everyone was now in a circle.

Aly snuggled up close to Brad. "It's *sooo* cold—come closer."

Amelia passed the weed over to Aly. She inhaled what seemed like half of the joint, and then grabbed Brad's face and put her mouth over his as she exhaled into his mouth.

Brad started coughing. "Whoa, Aly, I wasn't—*hack, hack*—ready for that."

Meanwhile, Amelia was flirting with Ty and Jayce. Clay was staring at them. He looked jealous.

Jessa tapped Bryn and whispered to her "Amelia is so inappropriate, and I also heard she has a drug problem."

"Who did you hear that from?" Bryn asked.

"Oh, everyone knows," Jessa said. "She's constantly taking uppers, and then she takes sleeping pills because she claims to have insomnia from studying too late. It's so dangerous. I hope she gets some help. Maybe we should have an intervention."

Bryn could tell Jessa didn't really care if Amelia got help…she was enjoying spreading the rumor.

Brad's cough subsided and he cleared his throat to get everyone's attention. "I have an idea—let's play a game."

Ty rolled the empty champagne bottle out in the circle. "Yea, we already got the bottle!"

Amelia's eyes widened. "I am totally up for spin the bottle!"

Aly, Jessa, and Bryn responded simultaneously: "No way!"

"Anything but that game. I only kiss one man," Aly said.

"That is not what I was going to suggest," Brad said. "Let's play Truth or Dare."

At that moment, Aly started breathing so hard her panting almost drowned out the sounds of the waves crashing on the rocks below. She looked at Brad. "Why would you suggest that game?" Her voice trailed off and her whole body was shaking.

Brad covered her with his jacket. "Aly, relax, just breathe…count to ten."

He helped her stand up. "Let's take a walk—everything will be okay."

That's when Jessa jumped up. "Should I come too? She gets like this when she smokes pot after drinking; it's just a bad reaction… It's happened before."

Brad motioned to Jessa to stay back.

"We'll be fine; there's water in the limo. Just give us a few minutes."

Amelia, who found her way back to her boyfriend's lap, wanted to keep the party going. "So, does this mean we can play Spin the Bottle?"

Clay pushed her off his lap. "Move it, babe—I gotta take a piss."

Bryn walked over to Amelia. "I think we should probably call it a night," she said.

Amelia smirked at her. "No, come sit with me, Bryn, please." Then she whispered, "Brad was right. You do look hot tonight." Amelia swept a loose tendril of hair off Bryn's face.

Bryn wasn't sure what to do. She's never been in this situation before.

"And don't worry, your secret is safe with me," Amelia said, in a sultry tone.

"What do you mean, *my secret?*" Bryn asked.

"It's a good thing for you we didn't play Truth or Dare," Amelia teased. "What if someone asked…'have you ever tried to make out with a teacher…or a T.A.'" Amelia scooted closer to Bryn. "Don't worry—it was only me who saw you try to kiss him tonight."

Bryn was about to explain herself, but Amelia was already convinced.

She put her finger to her lips. "Shhhh—if you ask me, he missed out." Amelia moved her fingers from her own lips to Bryn's and softly touched them. "Don't worry, sweetie. I won't say a word." Amelia retracted her hand and stuck out her pinky finger. She had long, almost sharp, acrylic nails. Her pinky looked like a mini manicured dagger ready to stab Bryn in the back. Then, Amelia locked her finger with Bryn's and whispered, "I swear."

CHAPTER 7

LAST DAY OF SCHOOL, CLIFFS VIEW HIGH, STUDY BREAK

While Bryn relives that night, she studies Brad's intense demeanor. He keeps cracking his knuckles. The crunchy sound makes Bryn cringe. Brad looks worried, just like he did homecoming night.

Bryn still wants to pry for more information. "After you suggested the Truth or Dare game, did Aly say anything to you when you went back to the limo?"

"Not too much, she was very drunk and stoned, but she was rambling about something that happened like a year or so ago …a girl was drunk at the lookout and fell off the cliff. She didn't make it."

"Was she there when it happened? Who was the girl?"

Brad shakes his head. "I don't know. Aly started to say something about how by the time paramedics got there it was too late."

Bryn nods, remembering the end of that evening. "And then we went home, and Aly fell asleep."

"Aly passed out," Brad clarifies. He is now looking off in the distance. "We pretty much stopped dating or hanging out, whatever we were, after homecoming. I really didn't think about it until Spanish class… and seeing the photograph of, well, you know."

Bryn nods her head and then realizes they've been talking for almost the entire break, and she still needs to go into Luke's class to try to get the video yearbook. She's kept a safe distance from Luke since homecoming. But Jessa and Aly are right: he has been notably flirty with her lately.

Bryn tells Brad she will talk to Aly and smooth things over. He hugs her and lingers a bit too long.

"Will I ever get my chance with you," he whispers in her ear. Bryn considers it for a moment and doesn't pull away from him like she usually does. She's been so preoccupied this year, a little escape from it all might be nice. Brad moves his hands down her back and then tightly grabs her hips. He pulls her closer and says, "You know I really, really like you."

Bryn looks down. "I can tell," she says. "But, I really, really, have to get going, let's talk after the pep rally this afternoon."

"Cool, looking forward to it," Brad says. He sits back down on the bench. "Yea, I just need a minute."

Bryn smirks and waves bye as she walks up to the classroom.

Luke is at his desk sitting with his back toward

Bryn and typing on the computer. He swivels around when he hears her walk in.

"Brad is still trying to win you over, huh? I got to hand it to the kid—he's consistent all the way until the last day of school."

"You saw that, huh? Bryn shrugs. "Yeah, he just doesn't quit. Well, I told him we'd talk after the pep rally...so, ya know, we'll see." She walks over to Luke's computer. "Listen, I..um..." Bryn is about to say something to Luke when loud chants start to blaze through the halls. A group of seniors are running by with a megaphone, cheering that the day is half over. They stop in front of Lukes class to shoot silly string on the windows.

"I um... really need to work on my speech," Bryn says.

Luke takes off his reading glasses. "You don't have it memorized by now?"

Normally, it is the class president who speaks at the final pep rally, but this year they did a "Student's Choice." One guy and one girl would give a three-to-five-minute speech. The student body elected Tyson Chen and Bryn Matthews, which is surprising since Bryn has only been at Cliffs View for her senior year. You did have to get nominated by a teacher and have a 3.8 GPA or higher.

"No, I mean, I do—I just want to get some final thoughts typed out."

Luke stands up and motions to his desk. "It's all yours. I'm going to grab a quick lunch. Do you want anything?" Bryn looks out the window. "What are they, drawing...is that...oh, gross," she says." Her classmates are making inappropriate designs with the silly string. "I've lost my appetite," Bryn says.

"Can you just lock up when you're done?" Luke asks.

"Sure, I'll only be like fifteen minutes."

Luke walks out the door and Bryn watches him turn left down the hallway toward the staff cafeteria. She sits at the computer and searches the desktop until she finds the folder titled "Yearbook." Bryn clicks on it and sees an image named "Video Footage."

She gets out her thumb drive and starts to download the file. It's going very slowly, 10%...25%... and then it freezes at 35%. Bryn hits "refresh" on the computer, not even knowing if that will help or not. But it does, and the status reaches 100%. Bryn grabs the thumb drive and slips it in her bag.

Bryn rushes out of the classroom and hears a loud voice, "Hey!" Luke is standing behind her.

She lets out a gasp. "Shit! You scared me!"

"Sorry, didn't mean to sneak up on you... Did you get everything done?"

"Yes, I'm just rushing to meet up with Jessa and Aly."

"I saw them standing by Ms. Día's class in the hallway; they look pissed. You think they'll go to the Pep Rally with you?" Luke asks.

"Of course—they wouldn't miss my speech... Well, maybe they would...but I know they won't miss seeing the entire video yearbook," Bryn says. More students run by throwing confetti along with more silly string. "Anyway, I've got to get going; see you in a couple of hours."

Bryn meets up with Aly and Jessa and hands Jessa the thumb drive. "Mission accomplished; it was on Luke's computer."

Jessa looks very pleased. "Good job, Brynny."

Aly starts her interrogation. "Didn't you need a code or password? Teachers, even T.A.s, don't just leave their files open. What did you *really* have to do to get it, ha ha."

Bryn decides to mess with them. "I told him I was tense and really needed a back massage before my speech, then we just made out a little—we didn't want to get caught."

Aly and Jessa's mouths drop. Then Bryn laughs.

"Of course, you didn't!" Aly gives Bryn a playful shove.

Bryn shrugs. "His computer wasn't locked."

The three girls walk into Ms. Día's Spanish class. She has left for the day and always leaves her classroom open. Bryn puts the thumb drive in and the three girls and huddle around the computer. Six wide eyes focus on the screen, staring into the faint outline of their own reflections like a black mirror into the past.

Jessa gets frustrated as random scenes starts playing. "Bryn, what is this? It looks like outtakes or something?"

"I'm sorry this was the only file; it's titled 'Video Footage.'"

Jessa moves closer to the screen as the video starts. It shows, what looks like the beach area at the Cliffs, but the shots are fuzzy. Then, Jessa points to the bottom. "Wait, look at that! It's her!"

Aly is confused. "Who? I don't see anyone."

Jessa leans back, arms crossed. "I'd recognize those tacky fingernails anywhere. I know who's behind this!"

Jessa stands up to announce her discovery. "Looks like Amelia De Leon is back and trying to get her revenge."

Aly scoots up closer to the computer screen. "Amelia? There's no way, I mean, well, she did think it was you that ratted her out." Both Aly and Bryn look at Jessa.

Jessa rolls her eyes. "How many times do I have to say it, it wasn't me! Well, whoever sent those pictures a week after homecoming to Mr. and Mrs. De Leon of their youngest daughter, drinking, smoking, and kissing her boyfriend, really did a number on her. Remember, the next week they sent her packing all the way to Mexico City," Aly says.

"I saw pictures of the rehab she went to," Bryn says. "It looked more like a luxury resort."

Aly is still staring at the computer and looks perplexed. "But I heard she is still in Mexico and dating an actor she met in rehab…Marco something."

Jessa points at the video. "C'mon, look—that is her hand in front of the camera. She has the resources to pull this off and a motive. She thinks we sent the pictures."

Bryn pauses the video and zooms in on her hand. "It's not just the nails; look at the ring."

Jessa claps. "Bryn, you're a little detective! That's the 'purity ring' she got on her quinceañera. Spoiler alert: she should not have been wearing white at her party…she was far from a virgin. She only wears that ring because it's covered in diamonds."

"Whoa, Jess, that's harsh even for you," Bryn says.

"Okay, okay, I never liked her, but I swear it wasn't me who sent her parents those pictures. Plus, the cops caught her on video stealing purses at the homecoming dance. The evidence was stacked against her. Now, it's time to send that Señorita back down south!"

Bryn, Jessa, and Aly decide to go talk to Clay after their fourth-period class. He and Amelia had tried long-distance dating for a month or so, but that fizzled out quickly. But supposedly they keep in touch.

"I need to stop at my locker first," Bryn says. "I'll catch up with you two in a minute." Bryn's heart starts to race. She needs to pull it together. It's just too much—the pictures, hearing the screams, and the secrets. Bryn takes a deep breath and steadies her hand as she twists the knob on her padlock: 5-2-8-3. The locker is jammed; it won't open. She wiggles the lock and pulls harder, putting her leg on the bottom for leverage."Ugh, what is going on? Why won't it… ah…budge?"

Jessa and Aly look back from the hallway when they hear her grunt. Then, the locker door swings open, and Bryn jumps back as sand starts to pour out, covering her shoes and piling up on the floor. There is something peeking out of the sand and Bryn bends down to look closer. She brushes the soft sand out of the way and screams.

Jessa and Aly run back down the hall. "What happened? What is that in your locker?"

"It's sand," Bryn says. "It's filled with sand...and *that*." Bryn points at the white object partially covered.

Aly looks down first. "Is that—oh my god...is it teeth?"

"It's a human jaw and yes, with teeth," Bryn says.

Aly turns her head. "I think I'm going to throw up."

"What do you mean, a human jaw?" Jessa asks. "That could be anything—an animal or part of a fake skeleton from a Halloween store."

Aly is hunched over and dry heaving. "It looks real to me."

"What are you, some sort of paleontologist now? This is all part of Amelia's sick prank!" Jessa yells.

Aly clears her throat. "I think you mean forensic scientist."

Jessa glares at her. "Forensic what?"

"Paleontologists study fossils, like dinosaur bones..."

"That's not what's important right now, Aly. Whatever. I'm not an expert on bones," Jessa says.

Bryn runs her hands across the top of her head. "I

just don't understand—this whole thing is a mess. I'm really starting to freak out."

"Don't worry, the janitor will clean it up," Aly says.

"Oh my god, Aly! Bryn is talking about the pranks or scare tactics, all this, not the sand mess," Jessa says. She puts her hands on Bryn's shoulders. "It will be okay, we'll figure it out."

"Have you guys opened your locker at all today," she asks. Jessa and Aly share a locker.

"No, why would I," Aly says. "I returned all the books yesterday."

"Aly, she means there could be something in our locker, like hers," Jessa says. She pushes Aly toward their locker, which is next to Bryn's, and steps back. "You check, hurry up!"

Aly stares at it for a moment. "Okay, okay, just...give me a second." She unlocks it and jumps back out of instinct. She shuts her eyes then peaks out of one. "Is anything in there, tell me, is it bad?"

Bryn checks the locker top to bottom. "No, all clear," she says.

"Whew," Aly says.

"This is freakin' ridiculous," Jessa says. "Let's go!"

"Wait," Bryn says. "What is that, by the... skeleton jaw." Bryn bends down.

Jessa and Aly step closer and look. "Eww, don't touch it!" Aly says.

Bryn pulls out a shell bracelet. "Weird," she whispers to herself as she twirls the bracelet between her fingers.

Jessa steps closer and stares at the bracelet. "It can't be," she says quietly.

"Can't be what?" Bryn asks.

"Nothing, never mind we just need to track down Amelia, this has gone way too far," Jessa says. "Let's just get to class."

The bell rings and causes all three girls to jump back.

CHAPTER 8

LAST DAY OF SCHOOL, MR. DECKER'S CLASS

Mr. Decker doesn't even make eye contact with Bryn as she walks in and heads to her seat. Maybe the sock gag gift was too much. Then she thinks about his ridiculous method of grading and decides he deserved it.

"What happened to you guys?" Brad asks. Apparently, he notices they're out of sorts.

Bryn starts to respond. "Someone filled my locker with sand, and then—"

Jessa interrupts and waves Brad off. "We got it under control now, we're fine."

Mr. Decker stands by the whiteboard and addresses the class. "Today, we are going to watch a longer portion of the video yearbook. This will be the last installment and then, during the pep rally, we'll play the entire version. After this part of the video is over you are free to visit among yourselves."

He starts it and then walks into his adjacent office and puts on headphones.

"Well, looks like he doesn't want to be here today either," Clay says so the class can hear. "Man, Decks is the best. I wish all the teachers were like him and would show us movies twice a week."

Bryn can't even muster up a response to that comment. She has other things on her mind. As they all watch the video yearbook, Bryn, Jessa, and Aly are anticipating the worst. But there doesn't seem to be anything shocking so far, except for the lack of clothes in all the pictures. The section playing is **Summertime Standouts**. Video clips and pictures of students during the summer: vacations, parties, and at the beach. Pop music plays, and the guys watching whistle at the gratuitous bikini shots of the same five girls that flash on the screen. Bryn didn't send in any revealing pictures. She doesn't want everyone to have a digital copy of her half-naked body at their fingertips.

The next clip is **Senior Standouts.** Again, the same five to ten people typically campaign for themselves to win. The categories desperately need a modern makeover; the only one related to academics is **Most Likely to Succeed.** The focus is on **Sweetest Smile, Life of the Party, Loveliest Locks,** and **Cutest Couple.** Jessa had campaigned for her and Conner to be voted cutest couple; back when all the students were voting, they were still together. They probably would have won without Jessa's pushiness, but she wanted to make sure. They did win, by a lot. But after homecoming and the cheating scandal, she had to change that. *"There is no way I'm going to be in my senior yearbook next to him; it will seem like a mean joke. Why would I want to look back at that. No way."* She got help hacking into the voting sheets and removed the **Cutest Couple** standout altogether and changed the votes for **Most Stylish** to her name.

Bryn knows the point of the standouts is to have fellow classmates choose who they think fits in those spots. But every high school has a group of students fixing the votes in their favor. No one ever says anything about it. But standing out, especially today, isn't always a good thing.

All eyes are focusing on the results. You can hear whispers throughout the class.

"I didn't think they would show this until the pep rally."

"Like it's a surprise, everyone knows who wins these; it's totally fixed."

Then it happens again. The screen turns to black-and-white, and those creepy letters pop up. Aly puts her head down. "Oh, no," she says. The letters are jumbled like some sort of word game, and then slowly start to make sense, revealing the first standout:

Most Likely to Murder.

Under the title is an unflattering picture of Jessa: she looks disheveled, and her eyes are tired and puffy, barely open. Sarcastic whispers start to erupt among the students; they obviously think this is a joke.

"I figured her for 'Most Popular'. Or maybe it's supposed to mean 'Most Likely to Murder...someone who steals my boyfriend.'"

Bryn looks over at Brad, who isn't laughing like the rest of the class. He is staring at Jessa. Her face is pulsating red, like a broken stoplight.

Aly grabs her hand. "Jessa, we need to talk to your dad, now!"

Jessa stands up. "This is bullshit! Amelia has gone way too far."

Before Jessa has a chance to storm out, the image flips around. It's a picture of a girl; who's about fourteen or fifteen. She is very pretty and has a big smile; it looks like a class picture. Then, under the picture, letter by letter a name begins to appear: **K..a..t..e.**

Aly gasps. "Jess, it can't be Amelia...we didn't even know her then..."

"Aly, shut up!"

Then, one last picture appears. It's of Jessa, Aly, and Bryn together on homecoming night at the cliffs. Below is a caption:

"Tell the Truth or Someone will Tell it for you."

Then the Cliffs View High emblem appears, and a scratchy, voiceover says: "The rest of your Killer Video yearbook will play in its entirety during the final pep rally."

JESSA RUNS out the door and heads down the hallway toward the fence by the front of the school, and both Bryn and Aly follow. The kids in the classroom can still see them out the window, but they are far enough away so no one can hear their conversation. Jessa starts yelling…but it's not coming from her: the sound is echoing from the school through the hallways over the loudspeaker. It's a recording. Jessa spins around. "Where is that coming from?" It's like a mashup of Jessa's voice. The loudspeakers emit random phrases. *"Just do it, don't be a chicken. You're all talk, all talk, all talk!"* Then it ends with the same long scream.

Bryn cannot hold back any longer. "Jessa, Aly, you need to tell me the truth now. Whoever is doing this for some reason has included me, and I'll admit there are events in my past that I have wanted to escape for a long time, but I realize it's time for all of us to tell the truth."

Jessa turns to Bryn. "We get it, Bryn— your parents got divorced, your dad is an alcoholic…but no one really knows about that, so here, you are a different person, one of us."

Bryn pushes back tears and grips the metal fence out of frustration. "Please tell me the truth."

Aly raises her voice. "We need to tell her!"

Jessa finally agrees. "Okay, I wasn't completely honest earlier today, but I am going to tell you."

Bryn takes a deep breath. It feels like she has been waiting forever to hear this. She lets go of the fence and sits down cross-legged on the grass, Aly and Jessa join her.

"Last summer we were hanging out at our party spot 'the lookout' on the cliffs. Aly's brother, Gavin, met this girl earlier at the beach. She was around our age but from out of town, and Gav thought she was kind of cute...I guess. She was practicing her cheer routine on the beach, and he invited her to come hang out later that night."

"Oh, he didn't just think she was cute...Gav really liked her," Aly says.

"Okay, whatever—can I finish?" Jessa says. "Anyway, she came and hung out with us before Gavin and his friends got there. You could tell she really wanted to fit in...and she kept drinking a lot of the Jungle Juice, you know, showing off."

"Jungle Juice, what is that?" Bryn asks.

Aly is quick to answer. "You know, it's spiked punch. Basically, fruit juice with rum or vodka... The punch is so sweet you can't taste the alcohol."

Aly leans in and continues talking. "Yeah, so my brother was totally into her. I have never seen him like that—he was head over heels after just meeting her! He normally is just a big flirt and girls fall for him; they hook up and then he moves on."

Aly nervously starts pulling weeds out of the dirt and glances at Jessa. "Sorry, Jess."

It's obvious Jessa's ego has taken a hit. "Like I even care. Plus, this isn't about your brother, Aly." She turns back toward Bryn. "So, the guys had a football initiation thing that night and they weren't there yet, so it was just the three of us."

Aly jumps in again. "But Gavin was so excited to come meet us, it was sweet; he kept talking about her. He was planning on heading over right after football."

"Aly, stop talking about 'how sweet' it was; he only hung out with her once. You are acting like it was love at first sight."

"I think it might have been," Aly whispers.

Jessa ignores the comment. "Anyway, so, she kept asking us about our cheer team and telling us how she made the Varsity squad for the next year as a sophomore …which we didn't believe, so we asked if she could do a roundoff, double back handspring, back tuck with a solid landing. So, I dared her to do it…and Aly said, 'Double Dare.' Once you get a 'Double Dare,' you must do it."

"So, that explains your reaction to the lipstick shade name in Spanish class," Bryn says. "And then what happened?"

"She was trying to show off, we didn't think she'd do it…but she did…and she lost her balance and fell. We called 911, but by the time they got there it was too late."

Bryn still has questions. "That's it? What do you mean, 'too late'?"

"Yes…it was a sad accident. But what could we have done? She fell and di…died." Aly has her head down and looks like a wounded shelter puppy, like she has something more to say but is afraid the Alpha dog may bark at her.

But then Aly speaks, her voice shifts to a solemn tone. "My brother was so upset. He said it was the first time he had a true connection, and he could see himself really being with her. He even finished most of his senior year from home and took off early to New York. He says it was just to get a head start on everything, but he was devastated. He almost blames himself, like if he was there, it wouldn't have happened."

Bryn realizes that is the most honest statement she has ever heard Aly make.

Jessa stands up with her hands on her hips and looks down at Aly who is still playing with the grass.

"Aly, your brother is a player. Those guys just get excited about something new and shiny…then it gets old. I'm sure he is doing fine." Jessa throws her hands up. "There you have it. I'm guessing somehow Amelia found out and is trying to set us up and change the story. Probably to make us look bad and get payback for me supposedly sending her parents those pictures."

"Did you do it?" Aly asks.

"Ugh, for the last time, it wasn't me! I'm going to go call my dad. I'll tell the office it's a family emergency," Jessa says. "This has to be a privacy violation or something."

"Wait," Bryn says. "I remember reading an article about how they put signs up after a girl who was walking alone slipped and fell. It didn't say anything about how you and Aly were there, or a party earlier?"

"When we called my dad, he advised us to just say we walked by and saw her fall. It would just be a useless investigation, plus we could get in trouble for underage drinking, and that would tarnish our clean record."

Bryn recognizes that "lawyer language" from Defense Attorney Price.

Aly is mostly silent as Jessa recalls what happened. Her lips are tightly locked, like a basement door waiting for the right key to open it and reveal the secrets inside.

"My dad will help us with this," Jessa says as she heads to the front office.

After Jessa leaves, Bryn hugs Aly. "Al, this is crazy—how scary for you to witness that type of accident. I can't even imagine."

Aly nods. "It was horrible."

"Plus, everything with your brother. I'm sure it wasn't easy having him leave early; I know how close you two are. I'm so sorry."

"Thanks, Bryn. It really has been so hard for me."

"Are you sure that is everything that happened?" Bryn asks. "Something just doesn't add up."

Aly stands up and wipes the stray pieces of grass from her skirt. "That's everything," she said.

Bryn stands up beside Aly. "Okay, so you two dared her to do that gymnastics move and she fell, that's it?"

"Yes," Aly says. "After she fell, we called Jessa's dad, and then he called 911."

Bryn takes a step back. "What did you just say?"

Aly stutters and looks to the left, a telltale sign she is not telling the truth.

"I…I mean, we called 911 and then called Jessa's dad, you know to come get us."

Bryn shakes her head. "That is not what you said."

Aly puts her face in her hands. "Bryn, you don't understand. You weren't there…I wanted to call 911 first, I swear I did…but Jessa thought we should call her dad, just to make sure our story all lined up." Aly is talking very fast. "He was right down the street and came in like five minutes. We were so shaken up."

"But if the girl was hurt, why not call the ambulance and then call Jessa's dad? It just doesn't make sense," Bryn says.

"You know how Jessa is—she took control, like she always does. It's not like a couple of minutes would have made a difference. We really didn't know what to do. Her dad thought it would be easier to just say he came to pick us up and as we were getting in the car, we saw a girl who looked like she was either tired or drunk walking near the cliffs and fell."

Bryn shakes her head in disbelief. "Mr. Price told you both to lie? Aly, if it was an accident, why not tell the police exactly what happened?"

"Bryn, it didn't matter—she fell, it was an accident, case closed. Who cares if the semantics are slightly different?"

More lawyer language from the great Grant Price. He probably coached them on what to say. Bryn remembers the name plate under the sign near the lookout. "I read about how Jessa's dad donated money to put the safety railing up. He helped with a big part of the restoration too, and the Price name has been on the 'Unstable Cliffs' sign ever since, right?"

Aly nods. "He wanted to make it safer."

"And wanted everyone to know how much of a philanthropist he is," Bryn adds. The sign is engraved with bold mahogany letters: "The Price Family." Then, underneath the obnoxiously large name, it says: "Enjoy Safer Sunsets."

"Please, Bryn, keep this between you and me. Jessa and I promised not to talk about the details, and I almost messed it up telling Brad what happened."

"Aly, if there is anything else, you need to tell me. Whoever is doing this has made me a part of it too. I am in the pictures. For some reason they think I'm connected." Bryn leans back against the fence. "We all need to be on the same page. How are there pictures and even a video from that night? There had to be someone else close by."

"That's the thing—no one else was with us and no one saw us there."Aly bites her lip and puts her hand across her forehead like she is trying to curb an emerging migraine.

"Maybe you just didn't see them, but someone saw you. Amelia, or whoever is behind this, has plans to show a lot more in the next couple of hours," Bryn says. "What about my locker...the sand and those bones, they looked real. And that bracelet, was it Amelia's?"

Aly shivers. "Jessa thinks it could have been hers, but...I don't know... why would Amelia do this? I don't get it."

Before Bryn can ask anymore questions Brad runs toward them. "It isn't Amelia," he says and hands Aly a magazine: *La Vida Bella.* "Amelia eloped with that actor guy, Marco Salvatore, last month and they've been on their honeymoon in Belize."

Aly grabs the Mexican gossip magazine. "Eloped? Looks like Amelia made sure the paparazzi was there."

There is a two-page spread of pictures of the newlyweds in honeymoon bliss, sunbathing and kissing in tropical paradise and not back in Cliffs View.

"Where did you get this?" Bryn asks.

"After Jessa stormed out spouting something about Amelia's revenge scheme and how she has been back in town messing with the video yearbook, Clay went to get the magazine to show us how it couldn't have been her."

There is another full-page glamor photo of the happy couple in a beach cabana. Below the picture is a closeup shot of the engagement ring. A beautiful five-karat floating round diamond, flawless and surrounded by princess-cut emeralds. The article says Salvatore designed it himself and wanted to include Amelia's beautiful birthstone.

"Clay took the news hard; he still has the hots for Amelia." Brad points to the picture of the ring. "But looks like she is officially off the market."

Bryn flips to the next page in the magazine. "And officially out of the country. It says after the honeymoon they are moving into an estate in Mexico City.

Marco will be directing a new movie and Amelia is making her film debut."

Aly grabs the magazine. "Let me see that. Jessa is going to be pissed. Not only is she wrong about Amelia being behind this, but her life after rehab is a freakin' fairy tale!"

Brad takes back the magazine. "Do you really think now is the time for a status competition between those two? Someone is trying to frame all three of you. It may have been Jessa's picture, this time, but they reveal more each class, and that creepy voice said, *'The rest of your killer class video yearbook will be shown at the pep rally.'* That is some serious stalker shit," he says. "Where did Jessa go, anyway?"

"She went to get in touch with her dad," Bryn says.

Brad looks past them and points over the fence. "Uh-oh," he says.

There are two police cars in front of the high school and Jessa is talking to the cops.

"Let me see," says Aly. She shoves Brad out of the way. "That's Detective Gates…you know Charles Gates; he's one of Jessa's dad's closest friends. Charles has known Jessa since she was a baby." Aly waves over and yells toward them. "Jess! Jess!"

Jessa puts up her finger, motioning toward Aly to wait a minute. Bryn watches the intense conversation between Jessa and Detective Gates. Jessa's arms are crossed, and she looks angry. Bryn can't make out what she's saying, but it looks like she is asking a lot of questions. Then something unexpected happens: the officer gives Jessa a hug.

"Maybe someone was hurt," Bryn whispers to Brad and Aly. She takes a few steps back. "We should stop watching. I'm sure she'll come back to talk to us, but it obviously doesn't look like she's in trouble."

Aly cups her ear and pushes it right up to one of the holes in the metal fence. "I can't really hear anything, but if someone died or something she would be crying hysterically, right?"

Brad looks disgusted. "What the hell is wrong with you?" He shakes his head. "Why would you even say something like that?"

Aly snaps back, "What is your problem? Bryn said it first; maybe someone got hurt. Why are you mad at me?"

Someone did get hurt, Bryn thinks to herself. *A girl died.*

Aly is shouting as Jessa jogs through the parking lot to the school. "What happened, what did Gates say?"

Jessa's face is stone cold. She doesn't look upset, just in shock. "My f…father was arrested. Gates told me they just took him in for questioning, but I shouldn't worry, that it is most likely a misunderstanding."

Aly hugs Jessa. "Arrested for what," she asks.

"He said it had something to do with alleged blackmail."

"Like in one of his cases, or like blackmailing a judge…like in *The Juror*?" Aly's eyes widen.

Jessa pushes Aly away from her. "This is not a movie, it's my life! I have no clue about anything having to do with blackmail… I'm being threatened in our video yearbook. I need his help and he is being questioned. Everything is so messed up!"

Bryn tries to calm her down.

"Jessa, we are all being threatened—you are not alone. What about your mom, can you call her to help with your dad?"

Jessa shakes her head. "Officer Gates called my mom first; she is still in Monterey for the Art Gallery opening. She's trying to get a flight home as soon as possible."

"I wish there was something we could do to help," Aly says.

"I might have an idea," Bryn says. She hesitates for a moment. "No…never mind I can't, it's too risky."

"What is it?" Jessa asks.

"We could get the other key to your dad's office and see if we find anything in there," Bryn says. "My aunt has a spare key she keeps at home."

Bryn's Aunt Rae works part-time as an intern at Mr. Price's Law Firm. Rae is Pre-Law at Southern California University and has just started applying to Law Schools.

"But I don't want to get Rae in trouble," Bryn says.

"Bryn, please…this could really help. I don't know what else to do. You said I'm not alone—this is happening to all of us," Jessa says.

Bryn thinks about it for a minute. "What do you think your dad's arrest has to do with the video?"

Jessa continues pleading. "I don't know, but we can't rule anything out. We need to do this."

"How are we going to get off campus?" Aly asks.

"Leave that to me," Jessa says. "Jenny is working in the office today and she loves me. I'll get an hour lunch pass for us, as long as we come back in time we're cool."

"Ok, this could work," Bryn says. "Rae has class until four. But we have to be quick. I want to return the key before she comes home."

"Of course, of course," Jessa says. "I mean, if you think about it, your aunt *does* work for my dad, so it really is in her best interest. She owes him big time for this job."

Brad still stands close by listening to the conversation. He steps up to defend Bryn. "Hey, Bryn is taking a big risk going behind her aunt's back."

"No, it's okay, Jessa is right; it was very important for Rae to get that job," Bryn says.

"Well, it doesn't look like Mr. Price will be on anyone's reference list if the charges pan out," Brad whispers, under his breath.

Jessa slugs him in the arm. "What did you say?"

"Nothing...just the pep rally starts at four-thirty. If you guys miss it, no graduation."

"Oh, we will be there, with the cops, ready to arrest Amelia for harassment, slander, and I'm sure there will be other charges to slap on," Jessa says confidently. With all the commotion, they forget to tell Jessa that Amelia is off the suspect list.

Brad hands Bryn the magazine to take with her.

"You ladies better fill Jessa in on the Mexico matrimonial."

Bryn rolls up the magazine for now. "Let's just get the pass first. We'll talk about Amelia on the way," she says.

CHAPTER 9

LAST DAY OF SCHOOL, MR. PRICE'S OFFICE

"How can Amelia be totally innocent? She must have something to do with it," Jessa says, as she drives her silver BMW out of the parking lot. "Read me the last page again." Jessa insisted that Bryn sit in the passenger seat on the way to her dad's office so she could read her every word of the article about Amelia.

Bryn recites it again. "Model Amelia De Leon wed actor Marco Salvatore in a private ceremony."

"Ugh, just stop, I can't!" Jessa cries. She speeds down Ocean Ave. "I know, I know; she has been in Mexico the entire time. Why are they calling her a 'model'?" Jessa points at the tabloid picture of Amelia in her bikini. "Those are fake, by the way."

Bryn tosses the magazine on the floor. "I think you should slow down and focus on driving," she says.

"Yea, I don't want to see any more cops today," Aly says. "Where are we going, you missed the turn?"

"We are making a stop at that gift shop where they have those tacky shell souvenirs. I want to find out if anyone bought an anklet recently," Jessa says. "Then maybe we can find out who put it in Bryn's locker."

"Wait, how do you know it's an anklet?" Bryn asks.

Jessa looks at Aly in the rearview mirror. They are both quiet.

"What aren't you guys telling me," Bryn asks. She pulls the shell bracelet out of her pocket. "You both looked more freaked out by this brace—I mean anklet than the creepy bones in my locker!"

Jessa parks her car in front of the small boutique. "Okay, so that girl Kate was wearing an anklet that looked like the one in your locker. But she was wearing it the night that she fell off the cliff."

"I think it *was* the same one," Aly says.

"It couldn't have been!" Jessa says. "Aly, you need to stop, you are totally paranoid."

Aly shakes her head. "You don't think someone could have found the body and the anklet and then---"

"And then what?" Jessa asks. "Took her jaw and the anklet and put it in Bryn's locker. Are you off your meds?"

The image of a body snatcher gives Bryn the chills. "Jessa has a point, there has to be another one like it," Bryn says. "But who and why would they have it?"

"I don't know, we never found out much about her. Gavin refused to talk about it," Aly says.

"Well, someone knows and obviously they want something from us or they would have gone to the police," Jessa says. "We just need to find out who, take care of it and move on with our lives."

Bryn, Jessa and Aly get out of the car and head into the shop. There is hardly room to walk inside. The aisles are stuffed with, knick knacks, t-shirts and hats with the Cliff's View signature sunset logo. The smell of incense pollutes the store and gives Bryn a headache.

The girls walk up to the counter. "Hi, excuse me, uh, hello?'" Jessa says. A woman with emerald green hair and wide rimmed glasses looks up from her book. "Can you tell me if you carry these anklets?" Jessa asks. "Bryn give her the anklet."

The woman holds it up and then quickly shakes her head. "No, we've never carried anything like this, it looks homemade. But there are some different options in the back, lot's of shell jewelry, if you want to take a look."

"Ha, no thanks. I'm not interested in any of the 'jewelry' you have here," Jessa says. The woman rolls her eyes at Jessa and hands the anklet back to Bryn.

"Well, that was a waste of time," Jessa says.

"We have to get going anyway, we still have to stop by my house," Bryn says.

The three girls leave the store and walk back to

Jessa's car. Bryn gets back in the front seat and Jessa drives off way too fast again. "Really, Jess," Bryn says. "Slow down."

Jessa ignores her and takes a sharp turn, the tires screech and she stops in front of Rae's condo. "What? We are in a hurry," she says.

Bryn's heart is racing after Jessa's crazy 'turn of terror.' *Maybe I should grab a helmet,* she thinks to herself. Bryn unfastens her seatbelt. " I'll be right back."

Bryn goes inside and grabs the key from a dish on the counter. She checks the clock, runs back outside and hops in the car. Bryn waves the key at Jessa. "Maybe we'll have better luck at your dad's office, than that store."

"I hope so," Jessa says.

* * *

THEY'RE ALMOST at Mr. Prices office when Aly unbuckles her seat belt and puts her head between the two front seats.

"So, I was thinking," Aly says.

"Oh no," Jessa says sarcastically. "C'mon Aly you set yourself up for that one."

"Seriously, it couldn't have been Amelia," Aly says. "Someone put this lipstick in my bag today. It's brand new; I would have noticed it before."

"You have so much crap in that purse, it could have been in there all year," Jessa says.

Aly shoves the brown leather tote between the

seats. "No, I got my bag last month it was just released," she brags. "I do like this lipstick shade." Aly plays with the small tube, twisting the bottom up and down. She looks at her reflection in the mirror and starts to apply the lipstick.

"Stop!" Jessa screams. "That's evidence!"

Aly flinches, smearing red lipstick down the side of her mouth, and then drops the tube on the seat. She wipes the side of her face. "You scared me. Thanks a lot—I'm a mess!"

"There better not be a stain on my seat," Jessa says. She stops her car in front of her father's private gate and pushes up her sunglasses to get a better look at the shaded numbers on the security keypad.

"It's your birthday, right?" Bryn says as she watches Jessa punch in the code.

"What? You know my birthday was last week."

Bryn points to the keypad. "No, silly," she says. "Is the code your birthday?"

"Yeah, right," Jessa scoffs. "It's 'Roger.'"

"Like, your dog Roger?" Bryn asks.

Jessa flashes an obnoxious smile. "Yes, the son he always wanted." Jessa presses 7-6-4-3-7, the numbers on the keypad that match the letters R-O-G-E-R.

The alarm buzzes and the gate slides open.

They drive into Mr. Price's private parking spot. "He loves that stupid dog so much it's sickening," Jessa says.

Aly makes her signature pouty face. "Oh Roger, he's such a sweet old dog," she says.

"Yep, Dad brought home the cutest little golden

retriever when I was six years old," Jessa says as she gets out of the car. "I thought I was getting a puppy, but he made it clear over the years it was his dog."

The girls walk through the back door into Mr. Price's office. Jessa does a quick sweep of the room. "It doesn't look like anyone has been here yet." She rifles through file cabinets and then sits in her father's chair. Jessa looks tiny behind the dark mahogany desk. It is massively thick, as if an entire tree was used to build it. Aunt Rae told Bryn he brought the table back with him from Brazil. According to Price that is where the best mahogany grows. Bryn and Rae joke about how he probably insisted on picking out which tree he wanted cut down for his desk. Bryn grazes her hand along the side of the smooth desk and down the legs. "Sturdy," she says. "We'd be safe under here if an earthquake hits." Bryn bends down. "We could all fit, with room to spare—hey, there is something under here."

Jessa dives under the desk. "Where?"

Aly follows her without hesitation. They find an envelope taped to the bottom of the desk. Jessa opens it slowly, like she thinks something might jump out at her. Bryn peeks over Jessa's shoulder, there is a flash drive and three carbon copies of checks made out to *Starry Night Productions*. The checks are each for $10,000.

Aly grabs the memory card. "Let's see what's on here," she says.

Jessa grabs it back. "I'll handle that, thank you."

Jessa takes the memory card and puts it in the computer.

"Don't tell me the password is also Roger," Bryn says.

"Nope, it's my parent's anniversary," Jessa says. She types in the date and unlocks the screen. The first picture flashes on the screen; then thumbnail images load, each one more shocking than the next. They're all shot in a sequence, so it looks like one of those cartoon flip books when all the images start to fit together. But those books don't typically reveal a murder scene…this does.

* * *

Jessa frantically starts pressing the escape button. "Why won't this close?" she says, shaking her head.

More pictures flash on the screen, and then one of the small thumbnail images expands to fill the entire screen. It shows the girl, Kate, landing her back tuck perfectly. She did not accidentally fall, like Jessa and Aly said earlier. The subsequent pictures all expand to full screen.

"What is going on?" says Jessa. "I can't turn it off!"

The next set of pictures shows what looks like a confrontation between Jessa and the girl, Kate. Then the computer freezes on the most telling picture of all: Jessa's hands on Kate's chest, giving an angry push. Aly's silhouette is standing in the shadows.

Aly takes a step back as if mirroring her same

position in the background of the picture onscreen, just watching it happen. But Bryn is standing right next to Jessa, a breath apart, close enough to feel her fear. The three girls stay silent for a moment. No words are necessary; the pictures speak for themselves.

Bryn speaks first. "How does your dad have these?" she asks.

"I don't know," Jessa says.

"Why does he have them and who took them?" Aly asks from the corner of the office.

"I don't know," Jessa says again.

Bryn grabs the envelope with the three withdrawal receipts. One is dated from just a few months ago."You are right, Jess, I think this is all related… Maybe someone was blackmailing your dad and now they want more money, or…"

Jessa interrupts Bryn, "or they will show everyone these pictures, where it looks like I pushed her," she says.

Bryn points at the picture on the screen. "Jessa, c'mon," she says. "It is time to stop with the lies."

"We were messing around," Jessa says, flinging her hands in the air. She looks at Aly. "You, remember, right?" Jessa continues defending the picture. "Okay, yes, she landed her fancy gymnastics move and I challenged her to do another one."

"You were taunting her," Aly says.

"What?" Jessa scoffs. "Are you kidding me?"

Aly retreats to her corner. "Well, you were," Aly says under her breath.

Jessa places her hands firmly on the desk and stands up. "She drank a lot of the Jungle Juice; I didn't force her."

"She didn't know it was spiked," Aly confesses.

"You double dared her, Aly," Jessa says. "Stop acting all innocent."

Aly screams back at Jessa. "But you pushed her!"

"I didn't think she'd stumble back and fall off the cliff!"

Bryn grips the desk for balance; the weight of their confessions causes her knees to buckle. For the first time, she is hearing the whole truth.

"I swear, Aly," Jessa says, "if I'm going down for this, so are you!"

"You two, stop," Bryn interjects. "You said it yourself: it is probably about money."

Aly walks over to the screen. "I don't understand this picture of *you*, Bryn. You didn't even live here then," She points to the black-and-white image of Bryn when she lived in Crescent Pine, the one that popped up during the first-period video.

"Whoever is doing this obviously has it out for all three of us," Jessa says. "Maybe they just assume Bryn knows about it too, since we are always together. It's probably more about us because Bryn's family doesn't have the kind of money to pay them off anyway," she adds. "Sorry, Bryn...but you know what I mean. Didn't Rae work here when the last check was cashed. Maybe she has info on who my dad was giving money to?"

"This seems pretty off the books," Bryn says.

"My dad trusts Rae; let's just take a peek in her office," Jessa insists.

Rae has an office she uses the two days a week when she works for Mr. Price.

Bryn hesitates for a moment. "Well, we have already come this far… Let's just be quick."

They go into Rae's office. Jessa shuffles through some papers, and at the bottom of the desk there is an envelope marked *Confidential.* From inside the envelope, Jessa pulls out three bank statements and a business card. *Photographer, Lawrence Huxley, Starry Night Productions.* They turn over the card and see an artsy black and white picture of the photographer in half shadow.

"Who is that?" Aly asks. "Huxley, like Luke…maybe it's someone related to him?"

Bryn turns on the desk lamp. "Let me see." She holds the photograph directly under the bright LED light, then drops it.

"No, *it is* Luke," she says.

Aly picks up the picture from the floor. "Wait a minute," she says. "How can you tell for sure? He is in the shadow and you can't really see his face."

Jessa rips it out of her hand.

"Ouch," Aly whines. "You gave me a paper cut!"

"I guess it could be him," Jessa says as she examines the picture. "But Aly is right for once; you can't really tell."

Bryn points to his picture on the business card. "Look at the scar above his eyebrow."

Jessa and Aly squint to see it.

"You're, right!" Jessa says. "But why would Luke do this?"

Aly still looks confused. "And who is Lawrence?"

"Oh my God, Aly, Luke...*is*...Lawrence," Jessa says, over pronouncing each word. "Am I speaking slowly enough for you?"

"Maybe it's not him," Bryn says.

"Of course, you'd defend Luke—it's so obvious you two have this awkward flirtatious thing going on," Aly says. "Maybe you're helping him."

"I'm just as surprised as you are," Bryn says. She looks at her watch. "We are running out of time; the pep rally starts in an hour."

Jessa puts the business card and the bank statements back into the envelope. "Why would Bryn point out that it's Luke in the picture if she was helping him?" Jessa asks sarcastically.

Aly stutters, "I...I don't know...maybe, uh..."

Jessa mocks her, "Maybe...uh, you should shut up. We are taking these back to school and confronting Luke, or whatever his real name is, to see what he knows."

"Jessa, we can't," Bryn says. "My aunt will know we snuck into her office to get them, and I'll be in so much trouble."

"Why don't you just make a copy?" Aly says as she points to the copy machine.

Jessa smiles. "Smartest thing you've said all day." She opens the lid and lays the business card and bank statements flat. "I'll make a few copies, just in case." Jessa presses the number 3, closes the top, and hits start. When the first page of copy shoots out of the machine, Bryn picks it up off the floor. Then the copy machine starts beeping.

"Out of ink," says Aly. At least it made one copy."

Jessa flashes a big smile, and for a moment it looks like she may say something nice. "Wow, you can count!"

"Give me the originals," Bryn says. "I want to put them back exactly how we found them."

Jessa nods and hands them to Bryn. "C'mon, let's get going, Bryn, hold on to the copy in your purse... Aly will most likely get lipstick all over it."

"Sorry, it was an accident. I'll pay to get your car cleaned, okay?" Aly says.

"Forget it," Jessa says. "We have more important things to deal with right now."

The girls walk out of the office and get back into Jessa's car. She glances again at the magazine on the floor by the passenger seat. Before Jessa starts the car, she slams her hands on the steering wheel. "I knew it," she says confidently. "Amelia is not completely innocent!"

"What are you talking about," Bryn asks. "We've been over it a hundred times. She wasn't even home—"

Jessa interrupts. "—Homecoming, that's it! She told me the next day, when we were all hanging out, that she had a secret about Luke, something she found out on homecoming night, but she never told me exactly what it was. Maybe this is it!"

Bryn knows the secret she's talking about. Amelia

saw Bryn and Luke almost kiss before he fell in the fountain. She wonders how much Amelia said about Luke.

"Did she tell you anything else?" Bryn asks.

"No, and the next week her parents sent her to that rehab."

"Maybe Luke sent the letter to Amelia's parents," Aly says. "You know, because she was a liability."

Jessa nods. "Huh…that could be it. He had to get rid of her."

Aly sits up a little taller in the backseat, happy to be back in Jessa's good graces.

Bryn is quiet for the moment. She doesn't want to reveal that *she* is the secret Amelia was keeping. But she feels there is no choice.

They pull back in front of Rae's condo and Bryn runs inside to return the key. She takes a deep breath and looks at herself in the hallway mirror, "time for some truth telling," she says. She decides to tell Jessa and Aly about what happened with Luke at Homecoming. Bryn gets back in the car and they drive back to school. When they pull into the parking lot, Bryn is ready to confess. "Wait a minute, I have to tell you guys something," she says with her head down. "The secret is not about Amelia and Luke…it's about me and Luke." She clears her throat. "I was talking to him by the fountain outside during the homecoming dance. You know how uncomfortable I was that night. Anyway, I thought we were having a moment and I leaned in to kiss him…and…"

Aly and Jessa's mouths drop open. "And what?" they say in unison.

"He jerked back, away from me…and that is how he fell in the fountain."

Jessa and Aly burst out laughing. "Oh Brynny, I'm sorry," Jessa says between giggles. "I swear I thought he liked you too."

"Well, Amelia and Clay came out as he fell, but Amelia told me that night she saw me try and kiss him."

"How embarrassing," Aly says.

"Yes, it was," Bryn says.

"Clay told us that you two were talking and then Luke tripped."

"He didn't see it, just Amelia," Bryn says.

"Oh, Clay would have told everyone immediately," Jessa says "He couldn't keep that a secret!"

Bryn continues her confession. "I'm sorry I didn't tell you both. I just felt so stupid and rejected."

"Well, you're better off," Jessa says. "I mean, now that we know he is a criminal and most likely blackmailing my dad and trying to get him locked up."

They get out of the car and head toward campus. Jessa is ready to confront Luke. "C'mon let's go have a talk with Mr. Huxley."

The girls walk through the gym, where everything is being set up for the pep rally. The principal is standing by the podium and shouts over to Bryn. "Looking forward to your speech Miss Matthews," she says.

Bryn stops walking, and Jessa and Aly crash into

her. "I totally forgot about my speech! I'm supposed to be in Room 14, for a meeting in five minutes."

"We got this," Jessa says. "I want to bust that, Lawrence!"

"Yeah," adds Aly as she puckers her lips. "We wouldn't want you trying to make out with him again."

"Ha, ha," Bryn says.

"Go get ready for your speech, Bryn—we'll catch up with you at the rally," Jessa says.

Bryn heads over to Room 14, while Jessa and Aly head in the opposite direction to Luke's class.

CHAPTER 10

LAST DAY OF SCHOOL, BACK TO LUKE'S CLASS

"I still don't get how Luke and Lawrence are the same person," Aly asked.

"Aly, I just can't even explain it again right now. I'll do the talking.Just don't say anything!"

They walk into the classroom. Luke is sitting behind his desk looking through some papers. Jessa points her finger at him like she has spotted the villain. "Oh Luke, Luke, Luke...or should I say Lawrence?"

Luke looks up. "What are you talking about?" he asks.

"We know it's you who is behind all the weird pictures showing up in the video yearbook," Jessa says. "Aly, Bryn, and I did a little digging in my father's office, and it looks like you were black-mailing him with some doctored pictures, and we have the proof right here!"

She puts her hand out toward Aly. "Hand me the evidence!"

Aly stays quiet.

"Give them to me," Jessa demands.

"Remember, you told Bryn to hold on to them," Aly says.

"Why didn't you remind me to get them!"

Luke stands up from his desk chair. "I don't know what type of scam you are trying to pull," Luke says as he walks around to the front of his desk. "But I don't know who Lawrence is and I don't know about any blackmailing." He looks at his watch. "You two should be heading over to the gym—speeches are starting soon. You don't want to miss your girl, Bryn."

Jessa gives him a sly smile. "Don't you mean *your* girl Bryn? We know all about how you tried to kiss her at homecoming, she moved away from you, and then you fell in the fountain."

Luke puts his hands up. "Wait—that is not what happened."

"Just shut up," Jessa says. "Here's how I see it: a pervy teacher takes pictures of girls, at night, at the beach, and then tries to hook up with one of his students. You've been plotting this for years! The media will be all over it!"

"Look ladies, there was an incident at homecoming with Bryn, but nothing happened."

"Tell it to the judge; we got you," Jessa says. "It's our word against yours."

"Okay, okay, I can show you proof I had nothing

to do with this. I found something on the video; it explains everything."

Jessa is intrigued. "What did you find?" she asks.

"Wait here. I'll get it from the back and show you."

While Aly and Jessa wait curiously, Luke runs out his back-office door and locks it. Then he sprints around to the front door and before Jessa and Aly can get to it. He locks them inside the classroom.

"Let us out of here!" Jessa yells and bangs on the door.

All the classrooms are closed, and everyone is on the other side of the school for the pep rally.

Aly throws a chair at the window. "I'll get us out of here," she says. It doesn't make a dent.

"Ugh, It's bulletproof glass," Jessa says. "You can't break it."

CHAPTER 11

LAST DAY OF SCHOOL, ROOM 14

Bryn sees Luke sprint down the hallway toward Room 14. He comes inside and asks for her, "Miss Matthews, a word outside, please…"

He looks angry or scared, maybe a little of both; it's hard to tell with him. Bryn follows Luke out of the classroom. Then, he grabs her arm and pulls her into the empty room at the end of the hall.

"Ouch, you're hurting me," Bryn says.

Luke shuts the door. "Come here," he says. Bryn stands still for a moment. Her heart is beating fast. She can't tell if it's from being afraid or excited. Luke pulls her close and they connect with an instinctive force like two magnets. Their lips lock and Luke spins Bryn around so her back is pressed up against the door. He tastes like peppermint and his scruff tickles Bryn's lower jawline. She tilts her head to the right and Luke kisses her neck.

"Wait...we... can't," Bryn says. She can hardly get the words out. Finally Bryn pushes Luke away.

"I know, I know," he says. "I broke a big rule." Luke smiles and inches closer. "But I've been so good this whole time."

"We don't want to blow an entire year's worth of work over a kiss," Bryn says with a sly smirk.

"Yeah, but it was a really great kiss." Luke pulls Bryn closer again.

She gives him a playful shove. "That was pretty hot, but seriously it's time to get started."

"About that...what exactly happened at Price's office?" Luke asks. "Jessa says you found evidence, a picture of me?"

"Slight setback... They wanted to go into Rae's office to search more," Bryn says. "Rae was hiding some bank statements for us and Jessa found them. I told her to put the originals back and we did; she made one copy."

"They said you have the copy."

"Shredded and gone forever, baby," Bryn says.

Luke smiles. "Good job."

"Where are Jessa and Aly now?" Bryn asks.

"Oh, another slight setback." Luke scratches his head. "I had to lock them in my classroom."

Bryn shoves him hard this time. "Why would you do that! They have to be at the pep rally!"

"I'm sorry, babe," Luke says. "I had to find you and figure out what's going on."

Bryn moves in closer to Luke and kisses him on the cheek.

"It's okay, I'll take care of it." She slips her hand around his waist and grabs the keys out of his back pocket. "Go get set up for the big show," she says.

"Oh man, I thought you wanted to play some more," he says and grabs her hand.

"This isn't just fun and games, playtime is over, babe, at least for now," Bryn says. "Plus, I have to go rescue my 'friends' and make sure they have seats right up front at the pep rally."

Luke puts his hands up in the air. "You're the boss, babe."

"Oh yes, I am." Bryn runs around the building to work up a sweat and then goes up to Luke's class. She hears Jessa and Aly banging on the door. Bryn unlocks the door and runs up to them, putting on her best shocked face. "Are you two alright?" she asks as she hugs them, hopefully for the last time ever. "I saw Luke, and he kept asking about the bank statements and the business card."

"You are a mess," Aly says. "Did he hurt you?"

"No, I'm fine…but I showed him what I had and asked him for an explanation. He grabbed them from me and said I should go check on my friends. I was so scared that you two were hurt, I ran and got the master key from the principal."

"He can't get away with this," Jessa says. "Let's go confront him. We'll make a scene and call the police!"

Bryn stops them. "We don't have the evidence anymore; we have nothing to bust him with."

"Except…" Bryn holds up a case labeled "Video Yearbook. Plan B."

"What is Plan B?" Jessa and Aly ask in unison.

"I asked Principal Marcus if I could introduce and start playing the video yearbook right after my speech," Bryn says. "She gave it to me."

"Let's watch it!" Aly tries to grab the video.

Jessa smacks her hand back. "Aly, we don't have time!"

"But if Bryn plays it, everyone will see what we did."

Jessa puts her hands in the air. "I'm done trying to explain things to her. Bryn, what's the plan?"

"I replaced it with the slide show Jessa made—you know, pictures from our senior year that she put together."

Jessa thinks for a moment. "Okay, okay, it isn't perfect, but it will buy us some time and at least it isn't the video Luke was going to show."

"I like it," Aly says. "Oh, do we have the picture of Brad's butt from homecoming on the slide show?"

Jessa turns to Aly. "Let's just go back to you staying quiet, okay?"

Bryn instructs Aly and Jessa to grab seats up close while she heads to the bathroom to fix herself up.

"Finally, this is it," she whispers to her own reflection in the mirror. "It's always been Plan B, Bryn's Plan."

CHAPTER 12

LAST DAY OF SCHOOL, SENIOR PEP RALLY, BRYN'S SPEECH

Bryn's been waiting a long time to reveal the truth. Now, Jessa and Aly sit right up front in the bleachers. Still unaware of who they're really looking for. Their feet tap the wooden planks beneath and wide eyes dart from side to side as if trying to avoid a predator's attack. The once familiar gray walls of the gymnasium are now covered with banners that bleed crimson and blue. Every inch of this campus is saturated in those school colors. Tacky decorations, like confetti and crate paper, are scattered across the floor and a ballon arch is loosely built over the stage. Every few seconds a balloon escapes and floats up to the rafters then "pops," causing everyone to flinch. The band blasts the senior song and the students sing along loudly and out of tune. Bryn's ears are ringing and she wishes she could turn down the volume or put the celebration on mute. She takes a deep breath. It's almost over. In just a few minutes the party will end...and this time there are consequences.

· · ·

Principal Marcus motions to the band to stop and taps the microphone. "Testing, ahem, 1-2-3," she says. A high-pitch screech follows her voice as the volume adjusts to the gym's speakers. "Good afternoon everyone, I know you've all been waiting to see the entire virtual yearbook."

The crowd claps and chants, *"Woo hoo, Yeah, Seniors, Seniors, Seniors!!!*

"Okay, settle down students. Maybe I'm old fashioned but there is nothing like a like a traditional printed yearbook to look back at over the years, so those will also be available to purchase after the pep rally," Principal Marcus says. "But because of a substantial anonymous donation to the film club, this year, we were able to do something different, to take a risk and roll the cameras on Cliffs View's Campus." She pauses for an applause but the students start yelling again: *"Just play the video, Seniors, Seniors!!!"*

"Quiet everyone, please," she says. "I'd like to welcome up, your class of 2005 elected speaker Bryn Matthews."

Bryn clears her throat as she walks up to grab the mic. She sees Luke in the far corner, standing exactly where he is supposed to be. Jessa and Aly are sitting directly in front of the podium. "First, I want to recognize someone very important to me, and without her I wouldn't be the person I am today," Bryn says. "I wouldn't even be here at Cliffs View if it wasn't for her. Actually, I should say, I wouldn't be here if it wasn't for... what happened to her." Bryn looks down at Jessa and Aly.

"My true best friend, someone who should be getting ready for her senior year of high school," Bryn says as she changes her tone. "She will always be in my heart: my sister Kate."

A picture appears on the screen behind Bryn. It is the same picture of Bryn that flashed on the screen during first period. Except this time, Kate is standing next to Bryn.

CHAPTER 13

TWO YEARS EARLIER, AUGUST
26TH, 2003

"The first one to spot the pier wins," Max Powell said. He drove the dark blue Subaru toward the freeway exit. The sign *Welcome to Cliffs View* was barely visible in the distance. "Which of my beautiful ladies will be the lucky winner this trip," he asked.

It was tradition to spend the week before school started with Aunt Rae in Cliffs View which was about a five-hour drive from Crescent Pine. The Powell family—Max, Susan, Bryn, and Kate—stayed at the hotel right on the boardwalk, south of the pier. Aunt Rae's apartment was a couple of blocks from the pier.

"What do we win again?" Bryn asked with a hint of sarcasm. She winked at her sister.

Kate smiled and put her head between the two front seats. "Yeah, Dad, isn't it up to twenty-five bucks?"

"No," Bryn said. "I think it's a fifty."

"Well, I'm on the lookout," Susan said. "I want seafood for dinner."

The first one to spot the pier got to pick where they ate dinner.

"We want Cheeseburgers!" Bryn and Kate said at the same time.

"What, are you two twins or something?" Max asked.

"Pretty much," Kate giggled.

"You just had to get Mom pregnant again, right after I was born," Bryn said.

"Gross, Bryn!" Kate covered her face out of embarrassment. "Now I've lost my appetite!"

Susan kissed her husband on the cheek and then looked back at Kate. "What can I say, these things happen, and it was the best surprise."

Bryn rolled down her window and inhaled the salty air. She pinched her sister and discretely pointed to the lights illuminating the pier as the clouds dissipated around it.

"On three," she whispered. "One, two, three…"

"There it is!" the girls said in unison.

"That's fifty bucks!" Bryn said.

"Hmm, you can have twenty each," Max said. "Plus, you two get to pick a restaurant."

"I have an idea," Kate said. "It has been such a long drive; you and Mom deserve a nice seafood dinner."

"What's the catch, Kitty Kate," her dad asked.

"I thought Bryn and I could go to that cool outdoor restaurant, on our own?"

"But sweetie, we always have dinner together," Susan said, pouting her lips.

"Mom, it is literally right across the street, and we aren't kids, we're fifteen!" Kate said.

Her mom reminded her: "Bryn is fifteen, Kate you still have a couple months."

Max put his hand on Susan's shoulder as they pulled into the beach parking lot. "A dinner with you sounds nice, honey, plus they'll be right across the street."

"Okay, okay," Susan said.

"Yay!" Kate looked just as happy as when she tried on her Varsity Cheer uniform last week.

"Why don't you two just meet us at the hotel after dinner? The reservation is under Matthews-Powell."

"Mom, why do you still use your maiden name?" Bryn asked.

"When your dad and I got married I wasn't ready to give it up…plus I think it has a nice ring to it."

Max smiled. "Your mother's a modern woman, girls; you have a great role model." He grabbed two $20 bills out of his wallet. "Here are your winnings; see you in an hour."

The girls walked across the street to the restaurant, while Max and Susan headed up the street.

"Be good girls, stay together!" Susan said.

"I promise." Kate held up three fingers and yelled back to her parents, "Girl Scouts' honor…we won't talk to any boys…unless they're really cute!"

The girls laughed and ran off before their parents had a chance to change their mind.

"Bryn, I had a great idea: if we meet anyone, you can be Bryn Matthews and I'll stay Kate Powell... We can pretend we're college roommates. Do you think they'll serve us margaritas?"

Bryn shook her head. "With the makeup and your obvious...growth spurt this summer, you look older, maybe you could pass for eighteen, but not twenty-one!"

"I'm halfway kidding; just thought it would be fun," Kate said.

Bryn nudged her. "How about I just keep being your sister, okay?"

"Fine, " Kate said.

The hostess sat the girls out on the patio.

Even though Bryn and Kate were only 11 months apart, Kate was fourteen going on twenty-one. There was a major change this summer; she couldn't walk down the street without turning heads. She started wearing makeup, but just enough to compliment her stunning features: high cheek bones, long auburn hair and the Matthews-side yellow/green/hazel eyes. You couldn't help but stare at them.

Kate was a dancer and gymnast. Their mom started the girls in dance classes right after they learned to walk. Bryn tore the sequins off her first leotard, while Kate tried hers on every night and twirled around the house. When the girls were around five years old, Bryn remembered their holiday performance. She ended up sitting on the ground the entire recital, arms crossed and scowled at the audience. Kate was poised and elegant, she was a natural crowd pleaser.

Kate made the Crescent Pine Varsity cheer squad. She would only be a sophomore next year. Sophomores never made Varsity. But during tryouts she scored higher than the juniors and most of the seniors, so they gave her an option of joining either team. She figured she'd go for Varsity and if it didn't work out, she could join J.V. Her goal was to get a college scholarship and as the only sophomore on Varsity, she would get noticed.

This past summer she had also caught the boy-crazy bug. Bryn didn't care about having a boyfriend, but Kate was on the hunt.

"Here, hold this," Kate said. She tossed Bryn her jean jacket.

"Um, what happened to the rest of your shirt?" Bryn asked.

"This is the style, Bryn. What, don't you like it?" Kate was wearing a short black and white skirt and a white off-the-shoulder crop top. She fixed her hair and put on a coat of lipstick. Then, flashed a big smile at her sister.

"Okay, Kate, I don't think *Teen People* is scouting for their cover model today, so can we get burgers and fries now?"

Kate laughed. "Let's add onion rings, too."

A group of kids around their age walked past them on the boardwalk. A couple of the guys turned around, most likely to get a second look at Kate. She smiled at the one with the biceps.

"Hey, we hang out right down there every day," Biceps said. He pointed at a beach spot near a fire pit. "You ladies should join us tomorrow."

Kate peeked over at the spot. "Maybe we will," she said.

"Cool," Biceps said as he held up two fingers. "Peace out, pretty lady."

"Oh my god," Bryn said. "Is he for real?" Bryn pushed her sunglasses up and grabbed Kate's hand. "I am not going to be your babysitter if you want to run after greasy high school guys. Besides, he was probably a senior—did you see his arms?"

"Yep, I sure did," Kate said with a big grin. "Bryn, relax…we are on vacation." Kate pointed over Bryn's shoulder. "Look quick, over there!"

"What? More boys," Bryn asked.

"No, it's the sunset, I think there's going to be a green flash," Kate said.

"The 'green flash' is a myth," Bryn said. "I've never seen one."

Kate smiled and looked out across the ocean. "Neither have I, but I know it's real," she said. "You have to believe in it, Bryn."

"I'll believe it, when I see it," Bryn said.

* * *

THE NEXT MORNING, Aunt Rae knocked on the hotel room door. The "End of Summer" 5K and Fun Run was about to start. "This is your wake-up call, Powells. Kate, Bryn, you two better be ready!"

Max and Susan were finishing their coffee on the back patio and Kate was in the bathroom. Bryn rolled out of bed and opened the door.

"Good morning, sunshine," Rae said. Bryn gave her aunt a big hug.

"Hi, Aunt Rae!"

Rae handed Bryn an onion bagel with tomato slices. "I brought your favorite."

Bryn yawned a "thank you" and put her breakfast on the counter. She opened her suitcase and pulled out last summer's 5K souvenir shirt, a pair of running shorts and tied her hair back in a ponytail. She knocked on the bathroom door. "What are you doing in there? It takes thirty seconds to get dressed for the run!"

Kate opened the bathroom door. She was wearing tight black running shorts and a purple sports bra that said "Varsity Cheer" in silver sparkling letters on the front.

"Seriously, Kate, a little glamorous for a morning run," Bryn said as she stuffed the bagel in her mouth.

"Hey, I'm proud to represent the Crescent Pine Varsity squad!" Kate kicked her leg in the air. "Go Eagles!"

Bryn chomped on her bagel and spun her finger in the air. "Whoopty-do."

Kate crinkled her nose. "Are you sure you want to go anywhere with that combination of morning/onion breath! Ewe!"

Bryn got close to her sister. "I looooove you." Her words wafted in Kate's face.

"Girls, behave," Rae said. "You both look incredible. Are you sure you are just in high school?"

"Told you," Kate whispered. "We totally look older."

Rae ran over to her sister, who came in with her husband from the adjoining room of the suite.

"Hi, Susie Sue," she said as she gave her sister a big hug. "I'm so happy you are here! And Max, are you joining us for the run?"

Max shook his head. "Not this time, my knee has been acting up, but I will be cheering for you ladies at the finish line."

"Okay, old man," Rae joked.

"Aunt Rae, can you braid my hair?" Kate asked.

"Yes, of course. Bryn, you want a braid too?"

"No, I'm fine with a ponytail."

Rae began styling Kate's hair. "So, Bryn, did you bring your guitar?" she asked. "Open mic night is tonight at that new bar & grill, and I hear they have some spots available." She winked at Kate.

Bryn noticed they were up to something."You didn't sign me up, did you?" Bryn asked. "What are you two scheming?"

"No, not yet," Rae teased. "But you are so talented, and I wanted to show you off!"

"I'm not sure," Bryn said. "It's different playing in front of my family than an actual audience."

"Well, how about we just go tonight and check it out," Rae said casually. "Bring your guitar and decide then."

"Okay, maybe," Bryn said.

* * *

BRYN LOVED TO RUN. It didn't even feel like exercise to her. She put in her earbuds, listened to music, and her body just knew what to do. She was on the Varsity High School track team.

Kate thought running was a form of cruel punishment. If any of the girls were late for cheer practice her coach made the entire team run a lap for every late minute accrued. But, the Cliff's View Fun Run was a tradition so Kate stepped up and tried not to complain. Aunt Rae set the pace for the run and the girls clocked a twenty-four-minute 5K. Max cheered them on as they ran. He even made a sign. It said: "You Go, Girls" with all their names. Susan laughed as they crossed the finish line. "He is just too much; it's only three miles," she said.

"He is sweet...and it's 3.2 miles to be exact," Rae said.

They grabbed their finisher medals and posed for the annual picture.

"Are you girls going to be okay for a couple of hours while your mom and I take Rae to get her new car?" Max asked.

Kate's eyes lit up. "I almost forgot—how exciting! Are you getting a convertible? Can I drive?"

"Sure... when you get a license," Rae said. "I'm not getting a convertible; I'm thinking a bit more practical...but I'm sure you'll still approve."

"Come pick us up and take us for a drive when you get it," Bryn said.

Rae, Susan, and Max headed to the dealership while Kate and Bryn walked back to the hotel. Kate pointed to a swimsuit boutique on the corner. "Bryn let's stop here, please."

"Didn't you pack three bikini's already," Bryn asked.

"Yea, but those are from last season, let's just take a quick look and try some on."

Bryn nodded. "Okay, fine."

Kate grabbed a bunch of different styles, all bright colors and wild patterns, while Bryn went with just a conservative black two piece. They both came out of the dressing room and looked at each other.

"Black again, Bryn," Kate said. She grabbed a lime green bikini out of her dressing room and handed it to Bryn. "I think you should try this one, it shows more cleavage."

Bryn recoiled. "No, way, I'm good with this one and you show enough cleavage for the both of us!"

Kate smiled. "Ha, ha, very funny. So, what do you think is it too...ya know, flashy," she asked while examining herself in the mirror.

Kate was wearing a turquoise triangle bikini top with gold trim that tied around her neck in a halter style. The bottoms were a bit small for Bryn's taste, but fit Kate perfectly.

Bryn walked over and stood next to Kate facing the mirror. "I'm pretty sure it was made for you," Bryn said. "C'mon, let's get it, no need to try on anymore."

Kate and Bryn left the store and headed back to

the hotel. Kate stopped in front of a coffee shop on the corner. "That place looks cute," she said. "Do you want to get a cappuccino or something?"

Bryn shook her head. "No, I don't want an eight dollar coffee...oh sorry a "cappuccino,'" Bryn said in her best "rich lady" voice. They both started laughing.

That's when two girls rushed out of the coffee shop and one bumped into Bryn and spilled coffee all over her. Bryn stepped back and tried to wipe the mess off the front of her new race day shirt. "Hey, watch it," she said.

"Ugh, my Espresso," the girl said. And they walked off. Luckily it was cold brew.

Kate grabbed some napkins. "They didn't even stop to look at us, what bitches," Kate said. "The least they could do is apologize." She held up her fists. "Should we go after them?"

"I just want to get back to the hotel and change," Bryn said. "No need for a beach brawl today."

"Are you sure," Kate asked. "I'm sure we could take them down."

"Oh I know, *I could* but what are you going to do with those skinny little arms?" Bryn pinched Kate.

"Hey, I've got muscles." Kate flexed her biceps. "That is what eight years of dance and gymnastics looks like."

"Sorry, sorry, don't hurt me," Bryn joked. They laughed the rest of the walk back to the hotel.

Bryn opened the door, took off her coffee-stained shirt and fell on the bed. She curled up between two oversized hotel pillows. "I'm so tired," she said.

"What? I'm wide awake. It's time for the beach," Kate said.

"How about we go in like an hour," Bryn yawned. "I just want to close my eyes for a little bit."

"Ok, how about you nap, and I'll go down to the beach and you can meet me in an hour." Kate pointed out the balcony window. "You can see the beach spot from here."

"Okay," Bryn said. "I'm setting my alarm."

* * *

"BRYN, wake up! Oh My God! He is perfect," Kate said. She threw herself down on the bed next to her sister.

"His name is Gavin, Gavin Lockwood—what a cool name!"

Bryn rubbed her eyes. "What time is it?"

"It's almost four o'clock; you've been asleep for hours."

"What? No way!" Bryn looked at the clock on the bedside table. It was 3:57. "I'm so sorry, I was exhausted... I thought I hit snooze, but it looks like I turned off the alarm."

Kate jumped up and danced around the room, like she was a little girl again.

"Bryn, didn't you hear me?" she asked. "It's fine, I'm not mad... Gavin and I hung out the entire afternoon."

126

"Who?" She yawned. "The one with the muscles?"

"Yes, but he is really smart too and we have a lot in common." She gave Bryn a big hug. "I'm so happy!"

"That's great, but how about playing a little hard to get, sis?"

Kate headed into the bathroom, "Hard to get? We are only here for five days, silly."

"Have you talked to Mom and Dad?" Bryn asked.

"They're still with Rae, signing paperwork for the car, then they're going to the restaurant. Kate peeked her head out of the bathroom door, "I think Rae is going to her place first to change."

Bryn sat on the edge of the bed and noodled on her guitar. "I want to go to Rae's place and practice a bit before the open mic. Hurry up and get ready," Bryn said.

Kate turned on the shower and shouted over the running water, "About that…Gavin asked me to take a walk on the beach with him. He plays football and they have late practices all week, but he wants to make time to hang out. So, I was thinking I would do that and then meet you at the restaurant. Then after…"

"Then after, what?" Bryn asked.

"After, we can go to the party that he invited us to!" Kate yelled from the shower.

"It's a beach spot by the cliffs where all the high school kids hang out."

Bryn started singing, *"Katie is boy crazy, boy crazy…"*

"C'mon, mom and dad would never let me go without you!"

Bryn continued singing, *"Kate likes a football jock and wants to give him a big kiss..."*

Then Kate added to the melody, *"Oh, pretty please, come to the party with me, Big Sis!"*

Bryn giggled. "Hey, we might have a hit song on our hands—maybe I should workshop it tonight." She went into the bathroom and grabbed her toothbrush.

Kate stuck her head out of the shower.

"Then after the open mic we will go to the party, right?"

"Yes, I'll go with you to the party," Bryn said.

BRYN SAT on the stairs at the base of her aunt's front deck. Her feet dangled off the edge and she let her flip-flops slide off. Sand nestled in between her tan toes. The shell anklet she wore caught the sunlight reflecting from the ocean and made it look like it was changing colors. There were two matching anklets at the jewelry stand on the way to her aunt's house. The lady who made them smelled like patchouli oil and sage. Her jewelry was mostly turquoise, but Bryn was drawn to the shell designs. The woman said that the anklets were almost the same, but up close you saw how each shell was slightly different. It reminded Bryn of her and Kate. So, she bought both. Her sister was with the boy she met earlier. *A romantic walk on*

the beach, how cliche Bryn thought. But Kate loved that kind of stuff. Bryn strummed her guitar while she waited for Rae to get home. She had no idea what car she would be driving, so each time she heard an engine coming her way Bryn popped her head up.

"That's definitely not it," she said to herself as a big Ford truck roared by. There were a few guys in the bed of the truck. They whistled at Bryn as the truck slowed down. "Hey sweetheart, you need a ride?"

Bryn waved them on. "No, thanks."

If Kate were with her, she would have flirted with them and asked where they were headed. Bryn hoped she would never get in a car with someone she didn't know, but it was hard to trust her sister's judgment lately.

The next car pulled around the corner and Bryn could tell right away it was her aunt's new ride. A brand-new shiny red Jetta. Bryn stood up and waved. Rae pulled into the parking spot. She rolled down her window.

"How did you know it was me?" Rae asked. "I didn't tell you what car I was getting."

Bryn smiled and peeked inside. "You've only been talking about that red Jetta, all-black interior with a sunroof, since I was ten! I can't believe you drove that old Pontiac for so long."

"Hey, my Sunfire was a great car—show some respect. We were very happy together," Rae said. "Plus, I got a nice trade-in value, so it's a good lesson to take care of your cars."

"I know, I know, but you are starting to sound like my parents," Bryn joked.

"Ha, ha. It's time for you to practice your song; let's go inside."

Rae sat cross-legged on the couch, white wine in hand, and swayed to the melody as Bryn played. "You are definitely ready to play in front of an audience," she said and clapped for her niece. "Just don't forget me when you're famous!"

Bryn bit her lip, "I'm already so nervous, just thinking about getting up on that stage. What is that trick…aren't you supposed to picture everyone in their underwear?" Bryn asked. "That just freaks me out even more!"

Rae laughed. "Yeah, all you need is a bunch of naked people staring at you! Honey, it's okay to be nervous. But if we never try anything new, how can we grow and become the people we are meant to be?" Aunt Rae always knew the right thing to say. Bryn didn't know anyone here and they were leaving in less than a week.

"Okay, enough practice," Rae said. She sipped the last drop of her wine. "Let's go!"

Bryn hesitated a bit, "I think I need a little more time."

"No you don't," Rae grabbed her hand and pulled Bryn up. "Let's go meet your parents and Kate… by the way, why didn't Kate come with you?"

"I'll tell you all about it on the way there."

* * *

BRYN'S PARENTS sat at a table right in front of the stage. The patio was packed, and it looked like a lot of people were already in line to perform. Bryn went up to the hostess stand where they had a sign-in sheet, it said: "Open Mic Full, No More Sign-ups."

"Well, looks like I won't be making my debut performance tonight," Bryn said. "Whew!" She wiped her forehead in relief. "That was a close one."

Rae had a big smile. "Don't worry about it, hon', I called ahead." She waved and winked at the hunky bartender. "He's a good friend," she said.

"I bet he is," Bryn said. "Now I see where Kate gets it from."

"What does Kate get?" Her sister snuck up behind them.

"Whoa, where did you just come from?" Bryn asked.

"Oh, I was just on the most romantic beach walk ever," Kate said. "And Gavin is teaching me how to surf tomorrow!"

"See Rae" Bryn said. "She's just like you."

"Okay, girls, let's go sit with your parents," Rae said. "And Bryn, you are up third."

"Yay, Brynny," Kate cheered. "This is such a great night!"

"Well, I don't know if I can compete with a cool surfer like Gavin, but I got you a gift at the farmers market." Bryn pulled the anklet for Kate out of her purse then lifted her foot to show Kate her own.

"I love it, and they match," Kate said.

"They *almost* match. The lady who made them

said how at first they look alike, but up close each shell is different."

Susan walked up behind her daughters. "They stand out in their own way," she said, "Just like my two girls!"

Kate sat down at the table next to her sister and put on the anklet. "It's beautiful!" She stretched out her long leg and pointed her toes. "Thank you, Bryn."

"We ordered a few appetizers," Susan said. "I just picked out what looked good and ended up ordering too much."

Bryn realized she hadn't eaten since this morning. That was all she needed, to faint onstage from starvation. She scarfed down a couple tacos. Cliffs View had the best Mexican food.

Rae pointed to the stage, "Look they are starting."

The first and second guys onstage were regular open-mic performers. They had fans in the crowd. Both played their electric guitars and sang covers of popular songs, so everyone was able to sing along. Bryn considered changing her song to a safer one rather than an original that she wrote.

The sound technician cued the second performer to exit the stage and the emcee took the microphone.

"Up next, Bryn Powell, who's just here on vacation but has already made a name for herself as a talented singer/songwriter...so, remember her performance tonight because I'm sure she will be back touring soon."

Bryn looked at her aunt. "What did you say about me...a tour?" Bryn whispered.

"It's just a little fun promotion," Rae said. "Plus, you are such a star, so own it and get up there!"

"Let's hear a round of applause for B.B. Powell."

Bryn whipped her head around and looked back at her aunt.

"Woo-hoo, B.B!" Her family started cheering.

Bryn hadn't been called B.B. since she was six or seven, when Bryn insisted on being called by just her first name. She was named after both her grandmothers, whose names both started with B: Bryn was from her mom's side and Barbara from her dad's. They couldn't decide which name would be first and which would be her middle name. So, her parents put both names in a hat and her mom just picked one. Bryn thinks her mom wrote "Bryn" on both pieces of paper. She never officially admitted it to the family but always had a suspicious look on her face when they told the story.

Bryn walked up the steps to the stage and sat on the designated bar stool. She cleared her throat and addressed the crowd: "This is an original song I wrote; it's about keeping secrets and trusting your instincts. It's called: "Pinky Swear."

From Bryn's first note she felt at ease, the music flowed and she was able to hit every note; the crowd was smiling, and her aunt gave her a thumbs-up as she sang along. It looked as if both her mom and dad were about to cry. When she got to the chorus of the first verse, the crowd cheered, and it didn't even faze her when she dropped her pick and had to start strumming with just her fingers. It sounded even better:

And the secrets you hide, held deep inside,
can't set you free
So what do you really want from me,
Is it too much to bear, have you lost control
I Pinky Swear to not tell a soul
A lock without a key
Is what you get from me.

BRYN FINISHED the second verse of her song and the audience gave her a standing ovation. They even shouted "encore, encore." But when Bryn stood up to take a bow her left sandal got stuck on the bottom foot rest of the bar stool. It wobbled back and forth. Bryn couldn't get her foot out. She toppled over and landed with a loud "Thud!" Bryn's mom and Kate ran up to the stage to check on her.

"Are you ok," her mom asked. "Did you hit your head, let me see?

"I'm fine," Bryn said. She looked down to avoid eye contact with anyone in the audience. "Let's just get out of here, now, please."

Bryn tried to stand up but immediately felt a sharp pain in her in her ankle. "Owe! I can't walk on it," she said.

Bryn leaned on her mom and Kate for support as she limped off the stage and out the back door. The crowd gave her another round of applause when they saw she was okay. Bryn still didn't want to look up, she was too embarrassed. Rae and Max followed them to the back patio. Bryn's dad grabbed a chair for her. "Let me look at it hunny," he said. "Does this hurt?" He tried to move her foot.

"Ouch!" Bryn screamed.

"Yep, you need an x-ray. It's already swelling," Max said.

"I'll get the car," Susan said. "The ER is close, we can be there in 10 minutes."

A few guys who were in the crowd, and obviously very intoxicated walked by and heckled Bryn, "Hope you are having a nice *trip*," they said and emphasized the word "trip."

Kate, Bryn and Rae flipped them off at the same time. Then, the entire family started laughing.

"What a bunch jerks," Rae said.

"Okay ladies, I guess I'll let that obscene gesture go, considering the circumstances," Max said.

Kate walked toward the back door of the restaurant. "Bryn, you left your guitar on stage," she said. "I'll go back in and get it."

"I didn't settle our bill either," Susan said.

Rae followed Kate. "I'll go in with Kate and take care of it," she said. "We will meet you guys at the hospital."

* * *

WHEN KATE and Rae got to the Emergency room it was packed. They checked in with the nurse at the front desk.

"Hi, we are here to see my niece, Bryn Powell. She came in with a bad ankle injury."

The nurse looked at her computer and pointed down the hall. "Room 122," she said. "Can you sign in here please?" The nurse handed Rae a clipboard.

Kate and Rae signed the visitor sheet and went to see Bryn.

Max was sitting in a chair and Bryn was on the bed. Her foot was wrapped and elevated on a couple pillows.

"We are still waiting for the doctor to read the x-ray," Max said when he saw them. "The nurse said it might take another hour or so. They are really busy tonight and down a doctor."

"I don't think it's broken. I already feel so much better," Bryn said. She slurred her words and her eyes were glazed over.

"Pain meds," Max whispered to Rae and Kate. "She's very relaxed. Susan went to go grab some coffee."

"I could use a cup," Rae said.

"You two take a break. I'll hang here," Kate said

Kate sat on the hospital bed next to her sister and straightened out Bryn's new anklet. "At least your right ankle still looks semi-normal," she said.

"Ha, ha," Bryn said. "I can't believe I biffed it like that, I'm so embarrassed.

"Yea, I would have been mortified!"

"Thanks a lot, sis."

Kate put her hands up. "You didn't let me finish. I

would have been humiliated and probably would make Mom and Dad drive us home tonight," she said. "But you don't really care what people think, you are cool without trying…and just, I don't know, have this natural way about you, like you can handle anything, and it draws people to you. Plus, that voice. I can't even sing the tune to 'Happy Birthday' in the right key."

Bryn put her head on her sister's shoulder. "Kate, I do care what people think; I just am not obsessed with it and don't let it control me…or…" Bryn started to nod off.

Kate pulled the cover over Bryn, grabbed her an extra pillow and cuddled close to her sister.

When Max, Susan and Rae came back to the room, Kate put her finger to her lips and whispered, "shhh, she's sleeping."

"Rae why don't you take Kate back to the hotel, we will call you when we know more. The nurse thinks it's just a bad sprain," Susan said.

Kate nodded and Rae said, "Please, call us after you talk to the doctor."

They left quietly so not to wake Bryn.

"What a night," Rae said. She yawned as they walked to the parking lot. "Do you want to drive?"

"Are you serious," Kate said.

"It's only a few miles, we don't even have to get on the freeway."

Kate jumped in the air. "Yes! Yes!"

Rae tossed her the keys.

When Kate pulled up to the hotel Rae smiled at

her and said, "I'm surprised we weren't pulled over for driving under the speed limit."

"I was just being extra cautious," Kate said. "Thank you, that was really cool."

"Do you want me to come in with you sweetie, and wait until your parents get back?" Rae asked.

Kate shook her head. "No, that's okay. I'm just going to watch some TV and go to bed."

"Oh, that's right you have a morning surf date," Rae said. "I heard you telling Bryn."

"Well, I'm not excited about getting up at 6:30 in the morning. They call it 'Dawn Patrol' surfing. But I am really looking forward to hanging out with Gavin."

"You be careful and call me when Bryn gets back if you're still awake," Rae said. "I love you."

Kate hugged her aunt. "I love you, too."

That was the last time Kate's family saw her alive.

CHAPTER 14

LAST DAY OF SCHOOL, PEP RALLY

Jessa and Aly stand up and look at both exits in the gym. Luke is blocking one, now with a police officer, and Rae is standing at the other end.

"Sit down," Bryn says to them. "I need to finish my speech and I'm sure everyone is anxious to see the video."

Jessa tries to make a run for it, but one of the officers detains her. "You need to take a seat, Ms. Price."

Jessa and Aly have no choice but to watch as Bryn begins to narrate. "On August 27th, 2003, two years ago, Mars was the closest it had ever been to Earth in the last 60,000 years—a planetary rotation that won't happen again for another 287 years. The footage you are about to see was all shot in one night, when an eighteen-year-old astrology buff set up his cameras at a secluded spot by the cliffs, ready to capture video of Mars in retrograde…but he wasn't prepared to witness a murder."

"You may ask yourself, what does all this have to do with the Cliffs View Senior Class?" Bryn asked as she looked at the expectant faces in the gym. "My sister snuck out from our hotel room, that night. She went to a small get together where she waited for Gavin, Aly's brother." Bryn points at Jessa and Aly, "but they harassed and taunted her, tricked her into drinking and…"

Jessa interrupts her and yells, "Bryn's lying, this is all a big misunderstanding!" Bryn holds up the remote and continues to address the crowd. "The camera doesn't lie and it caught everything they did." She presses play. "You're watching secret footage from that night, and it's a bit shaky, but look closely and listen to the conversation between Jessa, Aly and my sister, Kate:

'Did Gavin say when he was showing up?' Kate asks.

Jessa shrugs. 'Who knows? They're at the senior foot-ball initiation thing. When it comes to football, the team is at the mercy of the coach. Plus, I wouldn't get too attached, those guys are all players and I'm not just talking about football.'

Kate smiles back at her. 'I don't know about that, Gavin and I talked all afternoon at the beach, we really hit it off. He's also teaching me to surf tomorrow.'

Aly ran over. 'Whoa a surf lesson from Gavin, he has never done that for a girl before.'

Jessa rolled her eyes. 'Whatever, so are you really on

the Varsity Cheer team," she says to Kate. "Prove it and show us your skills, I dare you.'

'Yeah, Double Dare!' Aly says as she pours a couple drinks. 'Now you have to do it!'

'Here on the dirt?' Kate asks. 'I don't know.'

'C'mon, you can't turn down a double dare,' Jessa says.

Kate steps out of her flip flops and adjusts her new anklet. 'I don't want this to fall off.'

Jessa looks down at Kate's anklet. 'It has a double clasp...plus, your ankles are kind of thick, it won't fall off,' she says.

'Fine, just give me a minute to stretch,' Kate says confidently.

Jessa turns her back on Kate and walks over to Aly. She shouts back, 'hurry up, we don't have all night.'

Kate walks over to a softer flat part of the sand and takes off her anklet. She carefully lays it on a nearby rock. The camera picks up sound of her saying, 'I don't want it to break.'

"I'm ready," Kate yells over to Aly and Jessa.

Next, the video camera captures Kate launching into an amazing gymnastic move: a toe touch jump, into a double back handspring followed by a back tuck, which she lands perfectly.

BACK IN THE gym the students are intently watching the video and gasp, "Wow!"

Bryn nods in agreement with the crowd. "She was amazing, but keep watching."

· · ·

*'O*KAY, *now do a roundoff, back handspring, lay out,' Jessa says.*

Aly prances over to Kate. 'But first hydrate some more,' she hands her a drink. Kate smells it, 'I don't know if I should.'

'It's just fruit punch,' Jessa says.

Kate takes a couple sips. 'You know, I'm not feeling well. It's really dark, I'll just take a walk until Gavin gets back.'

'See, I told you, Aly—Katie was lying about making the Varsity squad as a sophomore,' Jessa says.

'I am not lying, and I go by Kate.'

'Then just do it—don't be a chicken,' Jessa says. 'Bawk, bawk, bawk!' She starts to walk away. 'It's obvious you were just trying to show off for Gavin,' Jessa says under her breath.

Kate strikes back, 'He mentioned your obsession with him. I know all about it and how he rejected you, more than once.'

Jessa turns toward Kate. 'What did you say to me?'

'Jealousy looks really bad on you,' Kate says.

That is when it happens. Jessa shoves Kate with such a force it causes her to stumble back off the cliff and fall into the low tide and rocks below.

T*HE* STUDENTS in the gym cover their mouths. Bryn's eyes start to water but she holds back her tears. "It's not over yet," she says. Jessa and Aly are gripping the benches as they watch themselves on camera.

.   .   .

ALY SCREAMS, 'WHAT DID YOU DO?!!' *She runs to the edge. 'I can't see her! Oh my god, we need to call 911, Jess.'*

Jessa is frozen. 'I didn't...think she was going to fall. We were just messing around.'

Aly nods. 'I know, I know; it was an accident. We'll tell the police, she just tripped.'

Jessa walks toward the edge of the cliff—it is a fifty-foot drop—she peers over. 'Kate was drinking.'

Aly steps closer to Jessa. 'We all had some of the punch you brought, but she didn't know it had alcohol in it.'

'What is that supposed to mean?' Jessa snaps.

'Nothing, nothing...I just mean the police are going to look into it, that's all.'

'We need to call my dad,' Jessa says. 'He will know what to do.'

Aly points at the ground. 'What about her shoes?'

'I'll take care of them.' Jessa grabs the flip flops and inches further toward the edge of the cliff. She looks down and hesitates for a moment. She looks back at Aly.

'What are you waiting for," Aly yells.

'Um..she..never mind, nothing,' Jessa says as she tosses Kate's flip flops over the cliff.

Jessa walks out of frame toward Aly, but the camera is still recording. Within five minutes, a car pulls up and Mr. Price gets out.

Jessa and Aly point to the spot where Kate fell.

'You two get out of here—the driver will take you home,' Mr. Price says.

* * *

BRYN PAUSES the video on the image of Mr. Price and grabs a microphone to address the Senior class. "Kate was holding onto the edge of the cliff, hurt but still alive, trying to yell for help. She still could have been saved. The closest fire station was two blocks away," Bryn says. "The first responders are experts when it comes to cliff rescues. Kate might still be alive today if Jessa and Aly would have just called 911 first, instead of only thinking about themselves."

The video fades to black.

The students in the gym are in shock and start to ask questions simultaneously.

"How could she..."

"Did you see that...and they covered it up for how long?"

"Did you know it was Bryn's sister?"

A police officer walks over to Jessa and the other corners Aly. Both are put in handcuffs and read their rights. Jessa screams at Bryn. "How could you do this, you crazy bitch!"

"Let me go!" Aly screams. She points at Jessa. "It was her; you all saw it! I didn't do anything," she says hysterically as the officer starts to walk her out.

Aunt Rae is standing by the exit. She steps in front of Aly and slaps her across the face. "That's right, you didn't do anything, and that is just as bad. You stood by, and watched; you are just as responsible." Rae turns her cold stare to Jessa. "And you, don't even think about trying to call your father," she says. "He is already under arrest and will be spending a long time behind bars."

"You were in on this from the beginning?" Jessa asks.

Rae steps closer. "Someone needed to get close to all the evidence," she whispers. Rae hands a folder to the detective. "I ended up uncovering shadier dealings involving Mr. Price, but this is the only murder."

"I am not a murderer!" Jessa yells. "It was an accident!"

Rae interrupts her desperate attempt at a defense. "It could have been, you could have called 911 right away and possibly saved her life, but the time you wasted thinking about yourselves instead of her needing immediate help, killed her."

Bryn steps down from the stage and stands next to her aunt. For once, Jessa is speechless. The officer escorts her out of the gym.

Luke begins to sidle his way next to Bryn. "So, should I go by Larry now?" he whispers. "Or do you like me as Luke?"

"Let's take a walk, *Larry*" Bryn says.

Before they leave the gym Bryn hugs Rae and whispers to her "give us about 10 minutes, okay." Bryn winks at her aunt and walks out with Larry.

"Do you remember when we first met," Bryn asks him as they walk down the hallway.

"Of course, I do," he says. "Accidentally running into you that morning was the best thing that has ever happened to me."

They walk a bit further and stop at the fence in front of the parking lot. "It's time you hear the truth. None of this was by accident," Bryn says. She opens the gate and points to the bleachers above the football field. "We should probably go and sit down."

Larry follows Bryn to the metal bleachers and nestles in close to her. " You know, there isn't anything you can say that will change how I feel about you."

Bryn stares off into the distance. "I'll start at the beginning."

"The days, weeks, and even months following Kate's death all blended together for me. I was living in a never-ending season of sadness. My family tried to attempt something of their usual routine, but no one could accept that this was now our reality. Rae stayed with us and took some time off from school. Our house was full, but I've never felt so alone. I remember looking at my mom a few days after the accident and saying to her:

'You will never be the same again, will you?'

Mom shook her head and then said, "None of us will."

My dad began drinking every day and no one addressed the issue, at least for the first couple months, and then it was just too late.

I was depressed, that was obvious. The guilt for not going with Kate that night haunted me all the time. But there was something else gnawing at me deep inside. I felt it in my gut. I couldn't shake the feeling that there must be more to what happened that night. I was obsessed with different scenarios and couldn't sleep. It was more than grief; I felt that Kate wanted me to keep searching for answers.

That's when my mom and aunt insisted I go to a therapist."

Larry interrupts Bryn, "Babe, I know all this, what more is there to tell?"

Bryn continues. "Please, let me finish. As you know Dr. Sandra Kane is a well-known trauma psychologist, specializing in teenagers. Her office is in Cliff's View, so I was staying with my aunt." Bryn starts to twirl her hair. "Larry, we didn't meet by accident, I knew you'd be there."

"The week before you saw me, I was in the waiting room, before my appointment. The man next to me was reading a local astronomy magazine. After he was finished, he tossed it down on the coffee table and I decided to flip through it."

Bryn turns toward Larry as she recalls what happened, her hazel eyes are like two solid agate marbles, with specks of gold that sparkle in between the green and blue.

"When I turned the page and saw the pictures I almost dropped it. That's when I realized the shots were from Cliffs View, and that they were taken on August 27, 2003, the same day as the accident... under the pictures of Mars, the location looked like the spot where Kate fell. Then, in the corner of the last picture: on the rock peeking out was a seashell anklet." Bryn crosses her legs and starts to fidget with her own anklet. 'The one in the picture was Kate's, I knew it. When the police called us after Kate's 'accident' I found her anklet by that rock. They said it probably came off when she fell, but that didn't make sense to me because it wasn't near the edge. Then I read the byline: *Photographer: Larry D. Huxley.* "I needed to find you, but I didn't realize how easy it would be."

"The man in the waiting room told me he knew the photographer, that he was a patient there too and he came in to the office Friday mornings at nine. That is when I switched my day and time so I could run into you...on purpose."

"I remember that first morning I saw you, you were sitting in the lobby reading the astronomy magazine," Larry says. "You know, I also didn't believe in therapy. My mom first had me go see someone after I started getting bullied in middle school. Larry touched the scar above his eyebrow. "The kids threw rocks at me. But talking about it really didn't help. I found my own method of therapy by becoming involved with astronomy. There was something very soothing about outer space and imagining something better out there. I thought I had everything I wanted; I was the youngest photographer to capture the photos of Mars in retrograde and they were published. I started the website, 'Starry Night,' and was doing well. I enrolled in courses to get my teaching certification. On paper, it may have seemed like I was doing great, but I had nightmares about that night on the cliffs." Larry grabs Bryn's hand. "But that all changed when I met you," he says. "That morning when I saw you, it was my final appointment with Dr. Kane. You asked me if I was the one who took the pictures in the magazine and that you recognized me from my bio."

Bryn remembers her performance. "I had to find out more about how you got those pictures and if you saw my sister there. So, yes, I set up our 'chance' meeting and invited you to have coffee with me after. It was sweet, we talked about how you were working on a portfolio to get into photography school and how I was in homeschool for my Junior year of high school. You were flirting with me."

Larry smiles. "How could I not, you're beautiful, smart, funny. I liked you right away. I remember we talked for a while...and then, that kiss. The moment we connected, the aching pain in my stomach started to fade away. Being with you was an adrenaline rush and it made me feel alive. It was like I was kissing the person I was meant to kiss. I felt how delicate you were in my arms and the longer I held you nothing else mattered. That's how I knew you were the one," Larry says as he scoots closer to Bryn and tucks a piece of hair behind her ear. "Do you remember?" He whispers.

"Of course," Bryn said. "I remember everything."

Larry puts his hand on Bryn's leg. "I was surprised that you made the first move because I was thinking about getting you alone from the moment I saw you at Dr. Kane's office. Don't you see, Bryn, everything finally made sense. Even if it was you who 'found' me it doesn't matter because we found each other."

"But that's when I decided to change the subject,"

Bryn says. "I wanted to hear more about the pictures you took and then I told you why: Cliffs View—was where my sister died, that past summer. The police said it was an accident she was walking near the edge and somehow fell."

Larry squeezes Bryn's hand tighter. "I knew I had to tell you everything at that point because when you said it was your sister, it all made sense, this was the way to finally make it right."

"I couldn't believe what I heard," Bryn says. "I wasn't prepared for it and had so many questions. *You were there... She was pushed... You saw who did it...*"

"I told you everything," Larry says.

"You did, every detail, more than I expected. The argument on the cliffs, the taunting, and even Mr. Price's blackmail. But the kicker was that you had a second small camera recording everything. Mr. Price didn't know about the extra copy, a mini DV tape, that you took with you that night."

"Bryn, I wanted to leave the coffee shop, go to my house and get the tape."

"After you said you had it all on tape, I saw my plan vividly and knew I couldn't pull it off alone. I needed your help."

Larry hugs Bryn. "And we did it! Come here, it's getting cold," he says. "That is why I did all this with you to try and make it right. "Remember when you tried to kiss me at homecoming and I jerked away because I saw Clay and Amelia coming out of the gym?"

Bryn laughs. "Yea you fell in the fountain for

me...and Amelia did see us, so we had to send those pictures to her parents before she blew our cover, it seems like so long ago." Bryn allows herself to lean into the nook of his shoulder. She rests her head on his soft sweater and shuts her eyes. For just a moment she lets everything go and feels at peace.

"You should be proud, babe, you executed a perfect plan, starting with getting the ditch day cancelled. All I had to do was bring it up at those PTA meetings and scare the staff with the underage drinking statistics." Luke says. "Plus, it was your clever idea to put a picture of Amelia's hand in those video clips, so Jessa and Aly would suspect her." Larry touches Bryn's cheek and moves his thumb to her chin lifting her face up to meet his gaze. "Hey, we did it together. If something or someone got in our way we dealt with it, nothing could stop us. I wish I could have seen their faces after you opened your locker today and found the skull and anklet. Hauling in all that sand was some serious work. But we stuck to the plan, we revealed the truth and everyone saw it. We got them, baby. I love you."

Bryn shakes her head and pulls away from Larry. "We didn't show everything...we didn't show you."

"Yea, but Bryn we had to delete the last part, where I'm behind the camera, talking to Mr. Price. It could incriminate me." Larry scratches his head. "Man, I could do some serious time."

Bryn looks Larry in the eyes and asks, "Do you know why I can't say 'I love you' back to you?"

"I know how you feel. You will say it in your own time," Larry says. "You've been through so much."

"Today before my speech, when we were alone in that classroom, I almost said it. I tried to picture a life with you. My feelings for you, over this past year, kept getting stronger. I mean, obviously, I am attracted to you and care for you as much as I can care for someone, after what happened. My heart is still broken and I know I'm not ready to truly love. But today, I thought maybe we can be together after all this. I was going to stay here with you and try to forget about the past."

"Bryn, what are you talking about? You *'were'* going to stay here*? Past tense?"* Larry asked.

"Listen, please, I need you to understand. When, I watched the video again with everyone in that gym I realized there is no forgetting or erasing the past. We could never have anything real."

"This is real," Larry says.

"I even called Rae and told her that I had changed my mind. 'Larry deserves a second chance,' I said to her. But after seeing it all again, I snapped out of it. You let Kate die. That is what's real. It can't be erased."

Bryn looks over Larry's shoulder at Rae who is in the media box above the football field with the police officers. "Sometimes I think Rae knows me better than I know myself. Even though I told her I had changed my mind, she brought the tape anyway."

"What tape?" Larry asks.

Audio begins to play from the speakers next to

Larry and Bryn. It's another conversation back at the cliffs but this time it is between Mr. Price and Larry:

'Looks like you have two choices, son: you give me this camera and all the footage, and you keep what you saw to yourself. Or should we discuss option number two?' Mr. Price threatens Larry, 'It's dark and dangerous out here, and sometimes photographers fall if they get too close to the edge. It's risky trying to get that perfect shot. Am I making myself clear?'

Larry pleads, 'I won't say anything, I promise, I swear.' Then more pathetic begging. 'Please don't hurt me, please!'

'Calm down, calm down. Give me the tape. I'll pay you to keep your mouth shut,' Mr. Price says. 'Come by my office this week, I'm Grant Price. You can't miss the build-ing, it's the big one at the corner of Peters St. and Santa Clara Ave. You were never here, got it, kid?'

Larry stands up and looks around the bleachers. "Bryn, what are you doing, why do you have this part? We erased it."

Bryn motions for an officer to come over. "I couldn't erase it. You are just as much to blame."

The officer approaches Larry. "Mr. Huxley, you are under arrest for accepting a bribe, withholding information, and falsifying documents."

"Wait a minute, Bryn, is this a joke, I...I don't understand. I love you and I know you love me too."

"This was never about love," Bryn says. "It was about the truth."

"But we've been partners this entire year—how can you do this to me?"

Bryn doesn't hold back. Tears fall down her

cheeks. "Partners," she whispers. She thinks about Kate and how she was her true partner. "How can I do this to you? You just watched as it all happened, and took the money and kept quiet. You'd still be keeping this secret, like Jessa and Aly were, and the footage from the second camera if we hadn't met."

"Bryn, I didn't have a choice," Larry pleads. "Price was threatening me."

"There is always a choice," Bryn says. "You could have ran over to check on the girl who was pushed off a cliff! You could have stood up to Jessa and Aly when they were taunting her. And you should have called 911 right away. You had a chance to save Kate's life. That is the type of man I would fall in love with. Why didn't you help her? How could you just stay quiet? Those questions haunt me every night. Even if it was too late to save her, at least you could have tried. Then we could have been together. But that is not what happened."

Larry puts his head down and the officers take him away. "I'm sorry," he says under his breath.

Bryn feels conflicted again, torn between Kate and Larry. Part of her wants to reach for him and kiss him. She realizes now, it must be love because it hurts so bad to let him go.

"I'm sorry too," Bryn says. "It's not the ending I wanted."

Aunt Rae walks over to Bryn. "You look like you're ready to get out of here," she says.

Bryn lets out a big exhale. "Yes, please." Rae puts her arm around her niece and they walk out to the parking lot. Rae unlocks the car. "It's over, sweetie. I knew we could do it."

Bryn get's in the passenger seat. "If I recall, you needed some convincing to go along with the plan at first."

Rae smiles. "Did I?" she asks.

CHAPTER 15

AUGUST 2004, 1 WEEK BEFORE SENIOR
YEAR STARTS, AUNT RAE'S CONDO

Rae sat on the couch and clutched a pillow in her lap. "No way," she said. "We are going to the police! "How do you even think we could pull this off, and why would you want to? If what you are saying is true, how could we just keep it under wraps for the next, what, ten months? This is insane."

Bryn paced the living room. "We can't go to the police," she said. "Price has them all in his back pocket. We need proof, so there is not even a small chance of them getting away with it this time or getting off easy."

Rae squeezed the pillow harder. "Bryn, this plan of yours, moving in here for the year, befriending those girls, getting close to them…how can you…? It will drive you crazy."

Bryn grabbed the pillow from her and put her hands on Rae's shoulders. "For the first time in over a year, I finally don't feel crazy or that I'm losing my mind. The 'accident' never made sense to me, I couldn't let it go, and deep down I knew there was more to it." Bryn sunk down on the sofa next to Rae. "This is the way for me to move forward. I know in my heart, it's the only way to take them down."

"I want to see the tape," Rae said.

"Are you sure? It is…heartbreaking."

Rae motioned to the television. "I know what it is, and I need to see it now. Please go get it."

The tape was in Bryn's bag. She wouldn't let it out of her sight. Not a chance. Bryn sat next to her aunt in silence as they watched what really happened that night. Jessa and Aly taunting Kate and then Jessa pushing her. Bryn knew what was going to happen, but each time she watched it she hoped for a different ending. Rae gasped and covered her mouth. Bryn didn't show her aunt the other part of the tape, the one from the small handheld camera that Larry had; that camera captured the footage when Kate was still alive after the fall, trying to hold on and yell for help. It was impossible to hear Kate's screams over the waves crashing, but she was still moving; they could have helped her. Finally, Rae moved her hands away from her mouth. "When do we get started?"

"Tomorrow," Bryn answered.

The next morning Rae and Bryn drove to the Price's neighborhood. Jessa lived at the top of a hill so they parked the car a few houses down the street.

There was a large oak tree that kept them hidden, but Bryn still got a good view through the branches.

"Hand me the binoculars," Bryn said. "They're in the bag in the backseat."

Rae laughed. "You seriously bought binoculars?" Rae handed Bryn the shopping bag.

"I've been watching them this past week to get an idea of their routine." Bryn said. "Check this out." Bryn pulled a platinum blonde wig out of another shopping bag. "It's part of my disguise."

"Where did you get this? Rae asked.

"That Halloween store, but don't worry I used cash, we can't leave a credit card trail," Bryn said.

"Wow you are in serious spy mode," Rae said.

"I borrowed Larry's car this week so I could tail them," Bryn said. She handed Rae a small notebook. "Let's review all the intel I gathered."

Rae began reading Bryn's meticulous notes. "Okay, Detective Powell, I'm on it," Rae said.

"It's *Matthews*! Bryn said. "I'm going by mom's maiden name as a cover, now keep reading."

Rae put her hands up. "Sorry, Bryn *Matthews*."

"It's ok, we just can't have any slip ups," Bryn said. "The first part of the plan is getting you on the inside: a job with Grant Price to gain his trust and access to proof of the blackmailing."

"Price isn't even hiring an intern at the firm. How am I going to get a job there?"

"You are going to rescue Roger," Bryn said.

"Who is Roger?" Rae asked.

Bryn handed Rae the binoculars. "His best friend."

Bryn pointed to the golden retriever in the Price's front yard.

"Our story is that poor Roger got out of the backyard and ran away. You find him when you are out on your mid-morning run. But, we are actually going to kidnap the dog...for a few hours."

"Okay, I get it," Rae said. "I say I 'find' his dog; he gets Roger back. But how does that turn into hiring me at the law firm?"

"It will be easy: say you recognized him, and you are pre-law," Bryn said. "Find a way to bring up how you have been looking for a job this fall. I know he will offer you something. Just mention one of his cases and tell him how impressive he is; that man loves flattery."

Bryn pointed to the house. "Every morning at nine the housekeeper takes the trash out the side gate," Bryn told Rae. "We have about ten minutes to get in and out, while the housekeeper walks to the other side of the house and trims the roses. She leaves the gate open. Roger is well trained and won't run out. But his one weakness is bacon. I learned about the bacon trick while I watched Mr. Price trying to get the dog into the car earlier this week. After we get Roger, we'll take him back to your place for a couple hours before you call the number on the collar. What do you think, aunt Rae?"

Rae scrunched up her nose and peeked in Bryn's purse. "I thought I smelled something."

"It's the good stuff, applewood smoked bacon. I couldn't go with a cheap kind, that dog is spoiled,"

Bryn said. "Look at them." Roger walked with Mr. Price to his car, sat and then lifted his paw.

"Did that dog just wave goodbye?" Rae asked.

Bryn nodded. "Yep."

After Mr. Price backed out of the driveway Roger ran through the 'doggy door' to the backyard. Bryn and Rae ducked when Mr. Price drove down the hill.

Rae popped her head up. "All clear!"

Next, the housekeeper walked to the other side of the yard.

"Right on schedule," Bryn said. "Let's go!"

RAE SAT with Roger on her back patio and rubbed his belly. "Oh, who's a good boy? You're a good boy, yes you are, oh yes you are." She nuzzled closer to his face. "He is a beautiful dog," Rae said.

Bryn patted his head. "Don't get too attached—it's almost time to make the call."

Rae looked at the fancy gold collar. "Let's get you home, Roger." Then she said, "You know, Bryn, we could get a small dog to have here... dogs are great for therapy."

Bryn grabbed the phone. "I went to therapy, remember? It worked. We are doing this because of what I discovered in therapy."

"That's not what I meant," Rae said. "Oh, I'm nervous. What if I say something wrong?"

"You'll be fine; do it just how we practiced." Bryn laughed, thinking about their role-playing scenario.

"Maybe not exactly how we practiced, but you know what I mean."

"Okay, I got this." Rae took a deep breath to mentally prepare. "I'm ready—phone, please." She dialed the number on Roger's collar. Mr. Price answered before the first ring finished.

"Um… hello, is this the owner of a golden retriever?…Yes, the name tag says 'Roger.'" Rae pulled the phone away from her ear as Price screeched with joy. "Yes, I have him; yes, he's fine… No, he is not hurt… Yes, I'll make sure, uh-huh…You're welcome, you're welcome… Yes, I'll stay here… I'm at 2214 Ocean Avenue." Rae hung up the phone. "He's on his way."

* * *

WHEN MR. PRICE GOT THERE, Rae recited the story perfectly. Bryn watched from the upstairs window. Rae told him how she was out for her morning run between study breaks, and Roger was wandering close to Ocean Boulevard. "He is the most beautiful dog I have ever seen," Rae said. She told Price about how she was applying to law schools and was looking for a job. Bryn saw Rae put her hand out, expecting Price to shake it, but instead he came in for a big hug. He got in his car with Roger and Rae walked upstairs. She waved the law firm's business card in front of Bryn and announced: "I start next week."

The next part of the plan was getting close to Jessa and Aly before the school year began. Bryn only had a few weeks. They had to form a friendship in the summer; it would be too hard trying to get into their circle after senior year started. Bryn had to do something significant, memorable, something that made her stand out.

Rae just put her notice in at The Vine; the internship would be taking up most of her time now, she wouldn't be able to waitress anymore. The restaurant was throwing her a going-away party; they even got Jasper Hall to come play. He was a local musician who recently made it big. Jasper was from Cliffs View and friends with the restaurant owner. He was also a favorite of all the local teenage girls.

Jessa and Aly stopped to get a latte at this bougie coffee shop close to The Vine almost every morning. That gave Bryn an idea. "Let's put a flyer up, about the party, in the coffee shop," she said.

"I'll have two of the girls in my yoga class do it and even hang out awhile to talk about how cool the party will be," Rae said.

Bryn pictured the type of members that frequented Rae's hot yoga class. "I'm sure they'll be perfect for the part."

* * *

THE NEXT MORNING, Rae sat in the back of the coffee shop while two of her fellow yoga students, Kim and Alexa, talked about the party with the barista. Aly and Jessa were standing behind them in line and Aly took a flyer that was left on the coffee bar. Rae could hear their conversation.

"Um, how did I not hear about Jasper Hall being in town?" Aly asked. She held up the flyer for the private show and party at The Vine.

Jessa pointed to the word **private**. "Maybe because it wasn't really promoted, Al."

"Well, that's a problem," Aly said. "It's invite only and we weren't invited."

Jessa threw her hands in the air. "When has that ever stopped us before? We are going."

Rae watched Jessa and Aly leave the coffee shop. Then, she went to meet Bryn who was waiting in the car across the street.

Rae got in the car and handed her niece a latte. "Worked like a charm," Rae said. She pointed toward the coffee shop. "Kim and Alexa look like Lululemon models and they were talking up the party while Jessa and Aly were in line."

Rae's friends wore those tight yoga pants that don't leave much to the imagination; they even called them "second skin." Which was a creepy marketing tactic, like they were manufactured by Hannibal Lector's leggings company.

"Jessa and Aly took a flyer, they were practically drooling over Jasper Hall," Rae said.

Bryn smiled at her aunt. "For someone who didn't want to get involved, you are really good at this."

"Well, if we are going to take them down, you can't do it alone."

"You know it's not just the two of us, Rae, we have some muscle too."

"Right, 'muscle.' How is Larry coming along?"

"Great. The film club donation went through, and Larry landed a T.A. position at Cliffs View. He will also be overseeing the video production, obviously."

"Okay, and what about, you know, telling him he needs to dramatically change his look so no one recognizes him? How's that coming?"

Bryn pulled out a photo of Larry from two years ago. He was chubby, with long greasy hair, thick-rimmed glasses, and acne. When Bryn met him he had sprouted four inches, his skin had cleared up and he replaced all that baby fat with solid muscle.

"Okay, so where's the 'after' picture?" Rae asked.

Bryn pointed to a table outside the coffee shop. "Meet Luke. The hot new T.A. at Cliffs View High."

Rae's jaw dropped. "Are you kidding me? Everyone was checking that guy out. I walked past him twice and had no idea."

"No one will—that's the point." Bryn said.

"I hope he keeps his cool around you. What if they notice something in class or, you know, if he gets too flirty?" Rae said.

"Believe me, he will be fine. You don't have to worry about La—I mean Luke; he's ready. He's a good boy," Bryn said.

Rae nodded. "Good job on the name, too; I like 'Luke' better than Larry."

"He picked it himself," Bryn said. "'Luke' is a nod to *Star Wars*."

Rae laughed. "Of course it is."

"Right," Bryn said.

"Okay, Bryn, you're up next. Are you ready? I don't envy you, sweetie; I mean, to hang out with those two every day without losing it, are you sure? Maybe we should move up the timeline a bit; we have the video. What about homecoming? I was thinking you could play the video at the football game or the dance; then you only have to put up this facade for a couple of months."

"Rae, that is not enough time for you to get what we need from Price. You need to gain his trust. The video shows what Jessa and Aly did, but not everything he did. We need proof of the blackmail. As for Jessa and Aly, they care so much about their senior year status and how they'll be remembered after high school. This will be the school's last memory of them. Plus, Jessa doesn't turn eighteen until June first.

Rae was pre-law so she knew what Bryn was talking about. "Bryn, you smart little cookie!"

"Yep, the one law Price can't get repealed," Bryn said. "Even though the crime happened when Jessa was a minor, she's more likely to be tried as an adult once she turns eighteen."

California was known for going easy on minors, but last year a law was passed that if the crime was severe enough, if there were special circumstances, along with the age at conviction, the chances of being tried as an adult was much higher. Even if Jessa was still charged as a minor, the sentence could be extended beyond a stay in juvenile hall.

"We got her," Rae said. "After we gather all the evidence and a jury sees the tapes, they will have to convict. They'll make an example of her."

"Now you see why we need to be in it for the long haul," Bryn said. "We are gonna take them all down."

* * *

WHEN JESSA and Aly arrived at The Vine, their names were not on the list.

"Just follow my lead," Jessa said. She walked up to the security guard, put her hand on his arm and gave him her best doe-eyed gaze. "Hi, Sean," she said, looking at his name tag. "So, silly me, we weren't sure if we would be back in time and tried to call and confirm, but the list was already printed out. The manager said he would write our names in. I'm Jessa and this is Aly."

Aly peeked over Jessa's shoulder. "It's Aly with a Y."

Jessa turned around and mouthed to Aly, *"Be quiet, you're not helping."*

Sean scanned the list and shook his head. "Who did you speak with?"

Jessa put her finger on her chin. "Hmmm, what was his name… I know it started with a *J*, or maybe an *L*." Jessa guessed.

"Do you mean Lisa? That's our general manager."

Jessa clapped her hands together. "Yes! Sorry, it

was Lisa. You know, maybe she has a cold or something, but her voice sounded manly on the phone."

"Well, let me go grab her; she is in the back—"

Jessa interrupted him, "No, I wouldn't want to bother her. We can sort it out later—I'm not upset."

Aly nudged Jessa. "Let's just go," Aly said. "This isn't working."

Sean stood firm by the patio door and held up the clipboard. "Look, ladies, you are not on the list, and—"

That's when Bryn walked up and tapped him on the shoulder. "Hey Sean, this is Jessa... *Jessa Price*. Rae is starting the job with her dad—that's why she is leaving, hence the big going away party."

"Well, they aren't on the list and we are at capacity. I am not supposed to let anyone else in."

"Oh c'mon, I promise we won't get into any trouble," Jessa said. "Well, maybe a just little," she teased.

Sean hesitated a moment and then moved to the side. "All right... but they are your responsibility, Bryn." He pointed at Jessa. "Keep an eye on this one."

Jessa winked at Sean, "Thank you!" They said simultaneously.

"You can thank Bryn; she vouched for you."

Jessa immediately hugged Bryn. The embrace shocked her. "Oh, hey, it's no big deal; you should be on the list anyway. My aunt is really excited to start working at the law firm next week."

Jessa smiled. "Yeah, I heard she saved his precious Roger. My dad will be indebted to her for life."

Bryn laughed. "Your dad was practically crying when he came to pick him up."

"It's weird, right?" Jessa said. "He's obsessed with that dog. Our housekeeper left the gate open and he got out. I was sleeping, but of course my dad blamed me for it."

"Why would he blame you?" Bryn asked.

Jessa shrugged. "Who knows, he is always on my case, I guess if Roger doesn't get his morning walk, he has too much energy. My dad said I was supposed to take him out," she said.

"Well, it sounds like it was just an accident, besides Rae found him and he is fine," Bryn said.

"Yes, they've been re-united and the world can go on," Jessa said sarcastically.

Bryn decided to change the subject and ask them about school, "Hey, do you go to Cliffs View High, by chance?"

"Yes!" Jessa motioned over to Aly, who was standing next to her. "We will be seniors. Where do you go?"

"I just transferred. I'll actually be going to Cliffs View, and I'm a senior too," Bryn said.

"You're transferring schools for your senior year," Aly said. "That sucks."

"Aly, don't be rude, you don't even know why," Jessa said.

Bryn smiled. "No, it's okay; there is just a lot going on with my parents and my aunt lives out here." Bryn waived at Rae. She was standing by the stage. "Plus, Cliffs View is such a good school."

"That's awesome, you get to live with your aunt; she's so young and pretty. My aunt is like 50 and smells like stale soup all the time," Jessa said.

"Do you even know anyone at Cliffs View?" Aly asked.

Bryn shook her head. "No."

Jessa grabbed Bryn by the arm. "Well, now you know us, and that's all you need!"

Aly looked around at the empty stage. "Hey, isn't Jasper Hall supposed to be playing tonight?"

"Yeah, he's in the green room," Bryn said. "You want to meet him?"

"Are you serious?" Aly asked. "Yes!"

This was Bryn's 'in' with Aly. "Well, let's go. We can get some pictures of the two of you," Bryn said.

Aly jumped in the air...she didn't even wait for Jessa to tell her how high.

After Aly and Jessa posed for a bunch of pictures with Jasper they sat at a reserved table in front of the stage with Bryn and Rae. Rae winked at Bryn and motioned to the restroom.

"We will be right back," Bryn said.

They walked to the restroom and checked the stalls to make sure no one else was there. "Well, it looks like you three are hitting it off," Rae said. "But how are you really doing with all of this?"

Bryn looked at her reflection in mirror. The person staring back at her was still broken, but the pieces were starting to come together and she felt stronger. "I'm good, just focusing on what needs to be done."

Rae fixed a piece of Bryn's hair that was out of place. "If it gets to be too much you let me know, okay?"

Bryn nodded. "School starts next week, it will go by fast and Jessa already offered to pick me up in the mornings."

Rae and Bryn walked out of the bathroom and watched as Jessa and Aly swayed to the music and sang alone.

Mission accomplished.

CHAPTER 16

Bryn sat on her porch and waited for Jessa to pick her up for school. Rae was already at Mr. Price's office for her first day of work. Jessa pulled her silver BMW into the driveway and honked. Aly was sitting in the passenger seat fidgeting with the radio.

Bryn got in the car. "Hi!"

Aly looked over her shoulder at Bryn, "So, first day at a new school, are you nervous?"

"A little," Bryn said. "Cliffs View is a lot bigger than my old school."

Jessa turned down the volume, "You have nothing to worry about, we are seniors, this year is going to be the best!" Jessa backed out of the driveway and hit one of the trashcans on the street. "Oops," she said.

"Did you know it took Jessa three times to pass her driving test," Aly said.

"Shut up, Aly, that DMV guy didn't score me right!"

Aly whispered to Bryn, "She ran stop signs during her test."

"It was one stop sign and I slowed down enough, no one was coming," Jessa said trying to defend her "rolling stop."

Aly held up two fingers and mouthed to Bryn, "It was two stop signs."

"Whatever, I passed and got the perfect car just in time for senior year," Jessa said. "Ugh, imagine how it would look if our parents had to drop us off, so you're welcome. Now, we can make a real entrance, get your cameras ready!"

Aly made a square with her hands and pretended to snap pictures of Jessa. "Oh, by the way, speaking of cameras did you hear about how this year they're making a video yearbook for the senior class?"

Bryn pushed her sunglasses up and leaned forward, "Yea, I did hear something about that...it sounds cool."

Jessa sped up to beat the yellow light. "Cool?" Jessa said. "Oh, it's going to be more than that, Bryn, it will be like a movie and we will be the stars! No one will ever forget us."

Bryn smiled. "I'm sure they won't."

Jessa parked in the first row of the school lot. "Prime parking is reserved for seniors," she said proudly as she turned off the engine. Cliffs View didn't have reserved parking spots for students but it was an unwritten rule that the senior students parked in the best spots. Jessa, Aly and Bryn got out of the car.

"It's going to be a great year," Aly said. "Plus, we have most of our classes together."

"Yea, because of me," Jessa added. "My dad has donated a lot of money to the school so it wasn't a problem to make a few requests. Except Bryn is *choosing* to take AP Bio and Advanced Calculus."

Bryn shrugged. "I like math."

"Ugh, why?" Aly Asked.

"It's not subjective, every problem has an answer. No grey area. You just have to put in the work and show all the evidence."

"Well, Bryn 'Math'-ews, ha ha, you're on your own," Jessa said. They walked toward their first class and Jessa stopped in front of the door. "Wait, who is that?" she asked.

Bryn answered, "That's probably, Luke the T.A."

"How do you know?" Aly asked.

Bryn pointed to the whiteboard. "It's written under Mr. Turners name."

"Oh, duh, but wow he's cute," Aly whispered.

Jessa pinched Bryn's arm, "He's totally smiling at you," she said.

Bryn laughed. "Yea right, he is smiling at everyone."

Aly turned around to face her friends, "See, I told you it was going to be a great year."

Bryn looked at Luke and then back at Aly and Jessa. "I'm sure it'll be a year we will never forget."

CHAPTER 17

LAST DAY OF SCHOOL, LATE AFTERNOON

Rae puts on a pair of sunglasses and ties her hair back in a ponytail. "Sunroof?" she asks.

"Absolutely," Bryn says.

Rae drives out of the parking lot. She tosses a letter on Bryn's lap. "So, I was thinking we head east."

It's an acceptance letter to Boston University School of Law.

Bryn smiles at her aunt. "You got in!"

"Yes, I did, and I found a great little house for rent walking distance to campus." Rae hands a large manila folder over to Bryn. Inside are brochures to Boston-area junior colleges. "You could start out at a J.C and transfer...maybe join me at BU for your undergrad," Rae says.

Bryn opens a brochure and starts reading.

"I talked to your mom; I know this is your story to tell, but your mom deserves to hear the truth from you and why this was your way to heal," Rae says.

Bryn nods and wipes tears from her eyes.

"Your dad is doing better too. He has been in rehab this time for sixty days. But your mom and the counselors agree that he needs one year of sobriety before they can fully reconnect if they decide to." Rae takes a slight turn onto Ocean Drive and parks by the beach. "The bench is ready," she says.

The family had a plaque made in memory of Kate and a bench dedicated to her. She loved poetry, especially the classics. Her favorite was a poem by Alfred Lord Tennyson.

Rae and Bryn get out of the car and take their time walking over to the bench, breathing in the salty air as they watch their footsteps imprint in the sand and then disappear with each gust of wind. Together, they sit on separate sides of the bench, so the marble plaque is between them. The middle was always Kate's spot. Bryn rolls up her sweater sleeve. She is wearing Kate's anklet as a bracelet.

Rae puts her hand on Bryn's wrist. "You finally took it out of the jewelry box," she says. "Kate loved it. She wouldn't want you to keep it hidden away."

Bryn unhooks the clasp and hands it to Rae. "No, she would want you to have it," Bryn says.

"Oh sweetie, I... I can't." Rae begins to cry.

Bryn stretches out her ankle. "It's ok. I already have mine. Put yours on."

They both sit in silence and look down at Kate's favorite poem imprinted on the plaque. The last bit of sunlight shines down, bringing the words to life. Then, the color of the sun changes from orange, to pink, to yellow and ends with a magnificent green flash. The first one Bryn's ever seen. A warm breeze gently touches Bryn and she feels lighter, as if a weight has been lifted from her chest so her heart can finally heal.

> *I climb the hill: from end to end*
> *Of all the landscape underneath,*
> *I find no place that does not breathe*
> *Some gracious memory of my friend.*

ACKNOWLEDGMENTS

First, thank you to my mom for... so many things it could be its own novel. For reading each version of *Pinky Swear* and yelling across the room to announce a typo. To my husband Geoff, my favorite person, who gives invaluable constructive criticism even if I don't like hearing it at first. My boys, James and Ben, thank you for letting mommy have her "computer time."

Thank you to San Diego Writers, Ink. and Tammy Greenwood's Novel Writing class. To Konstellation Press and Cornelia Feye for her professional polishing, which helped me to craft the story I've always wanted to write.

Finally, to my sister Brenna and brother Matthew thank you for the names that mold my main character.

ABOUT THE AUTHOR

Pinky Swear is the debut YA Novel by Kara Stevens. Her short story *White Rose* was published as a winner in the San Diego Decameron Project.

Kara lives in San Diego with her family. She loves spending the day at the beach with her husband and their two young sons. Besides writing Kara enjoys yoga, mystery books and movies with a good twist. Nothing makes her laugh more than reminiscing with her two best friends (of more than 25 years!) and recycling some of their crazy adventures in her fiction stories.